“How could you leave all this?”

Emma wiped her face again. Despite her disheveled appearance, there was a wide grin on her face.

“I know you don’t understand, but it wasn’t easy. Toughest decision of my life.”

Their gazes connected and Zach swallowed hard.

“Then why did you?” she asked softly. “We’d been friends since I was seven years old, and suddenly you left without a backward glance.”

He kept his mouth shut, unwilling to open that particular can of worms here and now.

“I guess there’s no point asking why you’ve stayed away for three years, either,” she continued.

When another heifer released a loud, mournful wail, Zach turned his horse around. “Saved by the heifer.”

“You can run…” Emma murmured. “But it seems to me that you and I have a lot to talk about.”

Yeah, she was right; eventually he and Emma were going to have to talk.

Why was it that although he’d never given a second thought to heading into danger as a navy SEAL, the thought of going toe-to-toe with his brother’s widow terrified him?

Tina Radcliffe has been dreaming and scribbling for years. Originally from Western New York, she left home for a tour of duty with the Army Security Agency stationed in Augsburg, Germany, and ended up in Tulsa, Oklahoma. Her past careers include certified oncology RN and library cataloger. She recently moved from Denver, Colorado, to the Phoenix, Arizona, area, where she writes heartwarming and fun inspirational romance.

Books by Tina Radcliffe

Love Inspired

Big Heart Ranch

Claiming Her Cowboy
Falling for the Cowgirl
Christmas with the Cowboy

The Rancher's Reunion
Oklahoma Reunion
Mending the Doctor's Heart
Stranded with the Rancher
Safe in the Fireman's Arms
Rocky Mountain Reunion
Rocky Mountain Cowboy

Christmas with the Cowboy

Tina Radcliffe

Recycling programs for this product may not exist in your area.

ISBN-13: 978-1-335-42837-0

Christmas with the Cowboy

This edition published by arrangement with Love Inspired Books.

www.Harlequin.com

Printed in U.S.A.

A man's heart deviseth his way:
but the Lord directeth his steps.
—*Proverbs* 16:9

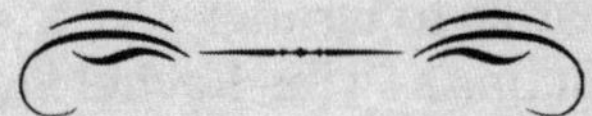

Book three of the Big Heart Ranch series is dedicated to the Big Heart Ranch Wranglers. God gives us the story and readers bless us by reading that story.

A special thanks to wrangler Trixi Oberembt, who named Emma's twins Rachel and Elizabeth, and wrangler Connie Saunders, who named the Big Heart Ranch Christmas celebration the Holiday Roundup.

A final bow to Rhonda Starnes for her helpful input, and to my deadline buddy on this book, SS.

I am blessed to have an amazing team that includes my agent, Jessica Alvarez, who is always on top of things, and the Love Inspired editors, including senior editor Melissa Endlich, who patiently mold me into the best writer I can be.

Chapter One

"Woo-hoo! Go get 'em, cowboy!"

Emma Maxwell Norman pushed a stroller with her two-year-old twin daughters closer to the Big Heart Ranch main corral, where hoots and hollers of excitement filled the air.

"Excuse me," she murmured while nudging her way past wall-to-wall people.

Western hats shaded faces against the glare of an early November Oklahoma sun, as the staff and kids of the children's ranch crowded next to each other atop rungs of the rail wood fencing. Eager children had even settled on the shoulders of adults to view the action in the main ranch arena.

Roars of laughter went up at intervals and heads turned left, then right, following the activity.

"Hey there, Miss Emma," Dutch Stevens said. The weathered cowboy tipped his hat and stroked his graying handlebar mustache. "Folks, let Miss Emma in."

The group of male and female wranglers stepped aside.

Inside the stroller, Emma's twins, Rachel and Elizabeth, barely stirred from their naps as another excited cheer went up. The toddlers had grown accustomed to life on the Timber, Oklahoma, children's ranch and thankfully could sleep through most of the noise inherent to a ranch that was home to sixty children.

At the far end of the corral, Emma's big brother, Travis, drove a small ATV in figure eights while pulling a dummy steer and kicking up a cloud of red dirt and sand. A rider straddling a chestnut gelding flew across the corral in an attempt to rope the steer.

There was no surprise at seeing her brother putting on a show, but who was the rider?

"What day is this?" Emma asked Dutch.

"Sunday, ma'am."

"That's what I thought." She frowned. "I didn't see an event on the schedule for today."

"Naw, this wasn't planned. Your brother and his friend are having some fun."

"They certainly drew a crowd."

"I'll say. That big feller on the horse is mighty good. Knows how to rope and he's faster than small-town gossip. He ought to go professional."

Applause went up as the horse and rider moved to the right and his lasso caught the bright green mechanical animal below both horns.

Then he smoothly dismounted, pulled off his navy blue ball cap and took a bow, displaying short neatly trimmed brown hair. There was something hauntingly familiar about the cowboy in the denim jacket and Wranglers.

When he turned to face the south side of the corral, Emma's head jerked back. For a moment, all she could do was stare.

Zach Norman was back.

A shiver ran through her, and she grabbed the weathered wooden rail for support.

Her brother-in-law. The last she heard, Zach was headquartered with his navy SEAL team in Coronado, California. Except for a brief visit after the twins were born, she hadn't really spent any time with Zach since the death of her husband, Zach's half brother, Steve, a little over three years ago.

"Miss Emma, you all right?" Dutch asked. "You're looking mighty pale."

Emma blinked and put a smile on her face. "Yes. I'm fine."

As she turned back to the corral, her gaze met Zach's. She knew the instant he saw her. His grin faded and the sparkle in his eyes was replaced by a shuttered expression.

Maybe it was the fact that they had different mothers, but Zach was nothing like his younger brother.

Both Steve and Zach were tall, with hair the color of toffee, though that was where any similarity between the brothers ended. Steve had clear blue guileless eyes. Zach's eyes were silvery gray. When he simmered with emotion, they became the color of the sky before a storm.

While Steve had literally been the boy next door, easygoing and laid-back, Zach could only be described as complicated.

Big, capable and brooding, he could steal your breath with one sweeping gaze. Although she'd known Zach since the day she and her siblings were plucked from foster care, there were times when she felt like she didn't know him at all.

When his gaze moved in her direction, it seemed he could see her soul. No one else could do that. Even now, as their eyes connected, she felt unable to look away. Emma swallowed and willed her pulse to slow down.

As he started across the corral, she noted a limp. Had he injured himself with his wild riding antics today?

Before she realized it, Zach stood in front of her.

"Emma," he breathed.

At five foot four, Emma had to look up over a

foot to meet his gaze. When she reached out for an embrace, Zach stood stiffly, arms at his sides.

"Welcome back," she murmured, pained at the rebuff.

"Good to see you," he said. "You're looking well."

"Thank you." She focused on his denim-clad legs. "You're limping."

"My knee. No big deal." He shrugged it off.

She frowned. It certainly didn't appear to be "no big deal."

"You let Travis talk you into the saddle when you have a bum knee?"

"That was my idea. Once I get up there, I'm fine. Riding isn't a problem." Zach's mouth formed a musing half smile. "You know, I don't think I've been in the saddle since…" He paused and met her gaze.

Emma instinctively knew what he was thinking. The two of them used to ride together when Zach stayed at his father's ranch. Steve had no interest in horses, but she and Zach shared the same passion for riding. Things were simpler in those days.

He looked away, his attention landing on the double stroller.

"Whoa! They've grown. Those last pictures you sent don't do them justice." Zach half crouched down next to his nieces, his hand bracing his extended left knee. "Who is who?"

"Elizabeth has a tiny birthmark on her right arm and Rachel doesn't. Other than that, they're identical."

"They look exactly like you," he murmured. Awe laced his deep voice.

"Yes," she said. The girls had her dark hair and brown eyes. "Except for their noses." As if on cue, Elizabeth wriggled her snub nose in sleep. "That's the Norman nose."

Zach nodded and offered a genuine smile. "So sweet."

"Sweet in slumber, yes." She couldn't help but chuckle. "And when awake, they're an Oklahoma twister doubled."

"Like me and Steve when I stayed with my dad in the summer." Another almost smile touched his lips as he stood slowly, favoring his left leg.

"When did you arrive?" she asked when he faced her again.

"Just got in this morning. Travis invited me for the wedding."

"The wedding was two weeks ago." Emma's glance went to where her older brother stood with his arm looped around his bride and assistant foreman, AJ Rowe Maxwell.

He shrugged. "I got hung up in red tape."

"Red tape?"

"That's right. Though, I suppose some might say that I'm trying to live up to my reputation as an absentee relative," he murmured.

Emma would not respond to the dig. It was a reminder of their harsh exchange of words via email regarding his lack of involvement in his nieces' lives.

"So you're here to visit?" she asked instead.

"You sure ask a lot of questions."

"Can you blame me? I've been trying to get you to the ranch for three years."

He shrugged and offered an annoyed sigh. "I made it."

"When are you due back?"

"I thought you were glad to see me." His eyes narrowed a fraction. "Now it sounds like you're trying to get rid of Uncle Zach."

"That wasn't what I meant." Emma's skin warmed under his scrutiny. Zach always managed to knock her off-kilter. She collected her thoughts. "I'm shocked, that's all. In truth, you were the last person I expected to see in that corral."

"Glad I could keep you on your toes." He offered a thoughtful nod with no hint of a smile to be found. "And for the record," he said, "the United States Navy and I have officially parted ways."

Confused and stunned at his admission, Emma stood staring for a few seconds. "Your knee. Is that why you quit?"

"Separation, not quitting. It was time" was his flat response.

Time for what?

Aloud she simply said, "Okay." Though, in truth, it wasn't okay at all.

While Zach's face remained expressionless, Emma's gut said that something wasn't right, and it involved his obvious injury. After all, this was the guy who ate, drank and slept navy for twelve years.

"What are you going to do next?"

"I'm tossing around a few options," he returned.

Her eyes widened as she latched on to his response. "You have RangePro. That's an option."

In an instant, he tensed. Then he glanced around. "Really, Emma? You want to do this here? Now?"

"We're only talking."

He rubbed the dark shadow of a beard on his jaw. "Talking, huh? Feels more like an interrogation."

"Don't exaggerate." She began to turn away, taking the stroller with her, when Zach's hand caught her arm.

"Emma, RangePro is Steve's company. Not mine."

She eased from his touch. "Legally, you're a partner. Fifty-fifty."

Zach met her gaze. "I haven't cashed a single check you've sent me. What part of 'buy me out' don't you get?"

"Did you look at any of the paperwork I mailed you?"

"I've been all over the globe the last few years.

I don't have the time or desire to shuffle through paperwork about a company I don't want anything to do with."

She took a deep breath. "The terms of the will state we own together or we sell together."

"Great. We sell. I'm sure the money will come in handy for you and your girls."

"It's not about the money. I am not selling what Steve worked so hard to build."

"RangePro was Steve's dream, and Steve is gone," he returned, his voice sober.

Emma bit her lip as she glanced down at her daughters, but she said nothing.

"Come on, Em. I'm not interested in RangePro and you've got to be way too busy with the ranch and the twins to run a livestock software company."

"If you'd give me a chance to show you—"

"Emma, it's a desk job. No way am I riding the range behind a laptop."

"That's not necessarily true."

"Not interested." Zach raised both hands. "And not staying long enough to care."

His eyes became steely and the set of his chin obstinate. The discussion was over. For now.

Frustrated, Emma turned away.

Three years after his brother's death and Zach was back. Though the thought of him being around permanently unsettled her, Emma would do whatever it took to save the legacy of her children's father. She knew what it was like to have your parents' memory swept away as though they never existed. No, she refused to be the one to auction off Steve's life work to the highest bidder, as though it meant nothing.

Zach tugged his leather gloves into place and adjusted the reins on the chestnut gelding. He had completely underestimated Emma. And her effect on him.

She was as beautiful as ever with dark tumbling hair that framed an oval face. If only he'd remembered not to look into her chocolate-brown eyes.

The moment he did, it was all over. He was lost. A teenager again, following her around like an overgrown Labrador retriever. The moment he realized that she had eyes only for Steve he'd respected her decision. Yet, that never stopped him from pining from afar like a sap. It wasn't coincidence that he joined the navy soon after Steve and Emma called to announce their engagement.

Although it was a secret he kept hidden, the truth was that he had wasted too much of his life in love with Emma. He refused to allow this trip to dredge up feelings he had purposely tossed overboard years ago.

Her entreaty from this morning echoed in his head, making him feel like a jerk all over again.

He was here and Steve was gone. How was

it his brother managed to shadow his life, even after death?

And why couldn't she let it go? *RangePro.* Like he needed another guilt trip. The irony burned and had dogged him every single day since the car accident that claimed his half brother's life.

The *whys* were doubling up on him.

Why was he still alive? Why had he made it out of Afghanistan and why hadn't his best friend?

God hadn't been forthcoming in the answer department of late.

Zach looked up at the jingle of tack and met Travis's smiling face as his friend approached on a black mustang.

"How do you like Zeus?" Travis asked.

"A little headstrong. So we're well matched."

Travis laughed. "Our equine manager, Tripp Walker, is pretty intuitive. He paired you up with a horse that suits your disposition."

"Quiet guy, that Tripp."

"To say the least."

"If you're the boss around here, why are you working on a Sunday?" Zach asked.

"I could give you a dozen reasons." He began to tick off on his fingers. "Getting married and going on a honeymoon put me behind on everything, for one. Then there's fall calving season. Oh, and preparation for the Holiday Roundup. That's gearing up here real quick, too." Travis shook his head. "I start my days behind."

"Holiday Roundup?" Zach asked.

"Christmas, pal. Huge around here."

"Today is the fifth of November. Thanksgiving is two and a half weeks away and Christmas is a long way off."

"Not when you're planning Christmas for every child who has made their home at Big Heart Ranch. These are abused, neglected and abandoned children. Many don't know what a real Christmas is. And I don't mean gift giving. The true meaning of the season."

"Who does the regular ranch chores while you're busy making all these Christmas memories?" He knew his voice sounded cynical, but his interest in Christmas was right up there with his interest in RangePro.

Travis nodded. "Nothing changes. We add the Holiday Roundup to our regular workload. Emma spearheads the entire project."

"Emma? Aren't her hands full enough?"

"Both of my sisters are without boundaries when it comes to the kids and Christmas."

Christmas. Zach squirmed. The holidays were nothing but a brutal reminder of the emptiness in his life. It had been that way since he was a kid. Pulled away from his father and half brother by a spiteful mother so he could spend Christmas all by himself. Yeah, one thing he didn't need was another reminder of the past.

"So, how many head do you have?" Zach asked, changing the subject.

"Up to one hundred now." Travis released a sigh. "And then there's the bison."

"You have bison? No kidding?"

"Definitely not kidding." Travis raised a hand and grimaced. "It's a long story. AJ is crazy about those shaggy beasts, and sometimes you do things you told yourself you'd never do all in the name of love."

Zach stared at him. "Did you ever think back when we rode on my father's ranch that one day you'd be telling me you were doing anything in the name of love?"

"I didn't know half as much as I thought I did in those days."

"How exactly did the cowboy who swore off love fall in love?" Zach asked.

"Not a clue. I sure wasn't looking." Travis offered a goofy grin.

Zach contemplated his friend's words for a moment and hesitantly asked the question pulling at him. "How'd you know?"

"Know what?"

"That she was the one?"

"The real question is how did I not know." He looked across the pasture to where AJ rode her horse checking cattle. As if sensing she was the topic of their conversation, his wife turned their way and raised a hand in greeting. In that moment, love shone in Travis's eyes pure and true.

Zach ached for what his friend had found. What would it be like to have his love returned unconditionally? To find a partner to face life with? He couldn't even imagine.

"You've got it real bad," Zach murmured.

"Terminal, I hope."

Zach chuckled.

"Quit your laughing. You might be next, so you better be careful."

He gave a slow nod. "At all times."

When Travis nudged his horse forward to inspect a group of heifers, Zach followed. Several had reclined in the pale brown grass and barely glanced up. "These mommas are ready for the whole pregnancy gig to be over," he observed.

"Yeah. Got a bent tail here," Travis said. "That cow is going to calve soon. We'll keep an eye on her."

Zach nodded.

"In a perfect world they'd all deliver in twenty-four hours and we'd be done counting calves before lunch tomorrow," Travis said.

"Good to have dreams, because my guess is that in the real world they'll be staggering delivery for the next two weeks and totally messing with your plans."

"You're right on." He turned in the saddle to face Zach. "Do you miss this?"

"When I'm praying to God that I'll make it out of a mission alive, yeah, I do."

It was more than that. More than he could ever admit aloud. He missed those summers on his father's ranch when he could pretend he had a normal family, instead of one where he was a bungee cord between divorced parents.

Zach leaned back in the saddle and inhaled the clean earthy fragrance of red dirt and golden autumn pasture grass. Seemed like he couldn't get enough. "In truth, I miss quite a lot about ranch life."

"You've got two months until you start the new job. What are you going to do until then?" Travis asked.

"No clue."

"Are you staying with your father?"

"My father has leased out the Pawhuska ranch. He's retired and is now circling the globe with my stepmother. Sort of a celebration because her cancer is in remission."

"I knew they were traveling on and off, but hadn't heard he'd leased. Any thoughts of taking over?"

"Never. Too many memories."

"I hear you." Travis frowned. "So where are you staying?"

"A bed-and-breakfast in Timber."

"That's no good. We have plenty of room in the bunkhouse. Why not stay with us until January?"

"Here?" Zach drew back slightly at the generosity of the unexpected gesture. "That's not a sympathy offer, is it?"

"No way. We're short staffed right now and having a jack-of-all-trades like yourself on staff to fill in the gaps here and there would help me sleep at night."

Zach adjusted his ball cap as he considered Travis's words.

"It's not nearly as exciting as being a navy SEAL, or staying at the Timber B & B, but we are your family. The plus side would be you get to spend the holidays with your nieces."

The mention of his nieces was enough to yank him right in. He was overdue for being a real uncle to Rachel and Elizabeth.

"I'm going to take you up on that," Zach said before he had a chance to change his mind.

"All right." Travis grinned. "Stop by human resources in the admin building tomorrow morning and fill out the paperwork. They'll get you squared away with a security badge to get you in and out of the gate."

"Will do."

Travis snapped his fingers. "Oh, and before I forget. Monday evening, 6:00 p.m. Big meeting at the Oklahoma Rose in town. In the banquet room."

"At a restaurant?"

"It's the staff Christmas party."

"Trav, I hate to beat a dead horse, but it's November fifth. You haven't even had a good frost around these parts."

"You're still not getting it. There's no time in December. This place has nonstop holiday activities from the day after Thanksgiving until Christmas Eve."

"I'm trying to understand," Zach returned, tucking away the information.

"You will, firsthand, and soon enough."

The pounding of hooves, announcing a horse and rider approaching in the distance, had both men turning around.

"Uh-oh, Emma found us." Travis raised his brows. "Or maybe she found you. Wait until she hears that you're staying."

"Could we keep his between us right now?" Zach asked. "Emma has her own agenda that I'm doing my best to dodge."

"RangePro, right?"

"How'd you know?"

"She's done nothing but talk about turning Steve's company over to you since you got back."

A groan slipped from Zach.

"Don't worry, your secret is safe with me. That said, this is a female-dominated ranch, so you know the odds of anything remaining a secret long are slim to none."

"Yeah. I figured as much, but if I can get even

a short reprieve from her trying to lasso me into her plans for my future, I'll take it."

"Have you suggested selling?"

"She's convinced that if she can tie me to a chair long enough for the RangePro spiel, I'll change my mind." He took a deep breath. "I'm telling you, your sister is the only woman I know who's as stubborn as I am."

Travis gave a chuckle. "I respect the fact that you admit that."

"That only means that one of us is going to end up very unhappy." Zach narrowed his eyes. "I'm committed to that person not being me."

"I hear you." He gave a nod toward his sister and called out. "You looking for me, Emma?"

"Yes. Dutch is bringing a breech to the barn and he needs your help." She pulled her horse up next to them and adjusted the black Stetson at the back of her head.

"Can you two monitor the rest of the herd?" Travis asked.

"I'm good." Zach nodded.

"Then I guess I am, too," Emma said as Travis headed back to the barn. The grim set of her lips and the expression on her face offered an uneasy détente. She'd work with him for the good of the ranch.

"Where are the twins?" Zach asked as his gaze skimmed over her. Despite the tension between them Emma was relaxed in the saddle. She wore a long-sleeve black T-shirt with the ranch logo on the front pocket. With a gloved hand, she pushed a single plaited braid of long dark hair off her shoulder. He stared, mesmerized for a moment, before returning to his senses and quickly averting his eyes.

"I've hired a sitter for a couple of hours every afternoon so I can help out, since Lucy can't ride," Emma said.

"Everything okay with your sister?"

"Apparently, you haven't seen Lucy yet. My big sister is having a baby."

"Whoa. Is everyone getting married and having babies around here?"

Emma laughed. "There does seem to be an epidemic, now that you mention it."

"Her first child?"

"Her first pregnancy. She and her husband, Jack, adopted triplets last year."

Zach opened his mouth and then closed it again. "I have no words."

"Most people simply say aw when they see seven-year-old triplets." She gave him a long look. "You're helping Travis out?"

"Yeah."

"That's hardly a vacation."

"In my world it is."

Emma shook her head and led her brown Appaloosa with white spots toward the outside of the pasturing herd. Zach followed, riding the flank.

"How long's this one been in labor?" she asked, pointing to a heifer reclining near the fence.

"Not long."

Silence stretched between them as they circled the pasture.

"Who's your App?" he asked with a nod to the Appaloosa.

"This is Rodeo." Emma patted the animal's neck as she continued to ride at a slow pace, eyes never leaving the herd.

"Rodeo? Does that mean you're still barrel racing?" Zach asked.

"No. I was never really much of a barrel racer."

"I thought you were."

Emma's face pinked at his words and she shook her head. "AJ is our resident barrel racing expert, though I try to get in some practice when I can. Sometimes I bring the twins to watch. I want to get them comfortable around horses right away."

"Good idea."

She pulled up on the Appaloosa's reins. "We have one dropping over there."

"Where?"

"There." She moved right and Zach followed. "The head is pushing through."

They held back at a distance, waiting and watching.

"Come on, little momma, you can do this," Emma murmured. "You were born to do this."

"There she goes," Zach said. The calf slid to the grass minutes later.

"That calf isn't breathing," Emma cried.

Zach's pulse kicked into overdrive at the alarm in Emma's voice. He made a clumsy dismount, forgetting for a moment that his knee had no plans to cooperate. Zach caught Zeus's saddle, barely escaping a face plant.

"Are you okay?" Emma asked as she, too, dismounted.

"I'm fine. Worry about the calf, not me."

Steps ahead of him, she slipped to the ground next to the calf. Pulling her shirttail free from her Wranglers, Emma swiped the animal's face, and then tickled the nostrils with straw.

The calf sneezed, spreading a shower of fluid all over her.

"Oh, yuck." She grimaced, wiping her face with her sleeve. "Thanks a lot, little guy."

Zach laughed. "Nice job. He's breathing all right."

Emma stood and backed away from the heifer as the mother sounded a grunt of protest and took over cleaning her calf.

"Whoa. Momma wants you out of there, Emma."

"Yes. I'm going." Emma moved and kept moving until she could grab Rodeo's reins and hoist herself back onto the horse.

Zach carefully swung his leg over Zeus's saddle, his gaze already taking in the rest of the herd.

"How could you leave all this?" Emma pulled out a bandanna and wiped her face again. Despite her disheveled appearance, there was a wide grin on her face.

"I know you don't understand, but it wasn't easy. Toughest decision of my life."

Their gazes connected and Zach swallowed hard.

"Then why did you?" she asked softly. "We'd been friends since I was seven years old, and suddenly you left without a backward glance."

He kept his mouth shut, unwilling to open that particular can of worms here and now.

"I guess there's no point asking why you've stayed away for three years, either," she continued.

Another heifer released a loud mournful wail and Zach turned his horse around. "Saved by the heifer."

"You can run…" Emma murmured. "But it seems to me that you and I have a lot to talk about."

Yeah, she was right. If he was going to be here until January, eventually he and Emma would have to talk.

Zach shook his head as he carefully headed toward the birthing cow.

Why was it that although he never gave a second

thought to heading into danger as a navy SEAL, the thought of going toe-to-toe with his brother's widow in Timber, Oklahoma, terrified him?

Chapter Two

Emma sluiced cold water over her face and arms, rinsing the evidence of a day's hard work into the industrial sink of the stables. She shivered and reached for paper towels to dry off. A glance down at her once shiny Ariat boots had her cringing. Something she didn't want to think about now decorated the hand-tooled leather. Rubbing the soles against a boot scraper in the corner, followed by the hard stomp of her feet on the stable floor, she managed to kick off most of the offending debris.

Though exhaustion dogged her, Emma's spirits remained energized. There was something satisfying about hands-on ranch work. She missed this. The last two and a half years had seen her cloistered in her office juggling the twins between therapy sessions with children and Range-Pro issues.

She glanced at her watch and then out the nearest window. The shadows of the day were closing in and she still had a riding lesson before she could head home to dinner and her girls.

"Miss Emma, can my brother, Mick, come with us for today's lesson?"

Emma turned to meet the hopeful gaze of Benjie Brewer, a ten-year-old with bright red curls and a round face. She resisted the urge to correct his grammar. Her sister, Lucy, was a grammar stickler, whose comeback when they were growing up was always *I don't know,* can *you?*

Emma favored example as the better teacher. "Isn't Mick on the schedule?"

"Yes. With Mr. Travis, but he's still working with some sickly calves in the barn."

"I can take Travis's lesson."

The familiar deep rumbling voice had Emma whirling around. Her eyes widened at the sight of Zach standing in the doorway. With his shoulders nearly blocking the sun behind him, the man seemed larger and twice as imposing as usual.

His gait was slower and the limp more pronounced as he closed the distance between them. Her gaze went to his face. The tight jaw clearly said that he was in pain.

After four hours in and out of the saddle with calf birthing in the pasture, she was in pain, as well. But she knew her minor aches were nothing compared to Zach's and yet he continued to soldier through. What drove the man?

"That work for you, Miss Emma?" he asked as he swiped at his brow with the back of his hand.

With a pointed gaze at his knee, she raised a brow in question.

"The knee is fine."

"If you say so," she murmured.

"And I do."

Emma took off her Stetson and pushed damp and tangled strands of hair from her face before sliding the hat to the back of her head. "Mr. Zach, this is Benjie Brewer. His brother is no doubt hiding around the corner."

"Mick, you can come out now," Benjie called.

Where Benjie was pale, short and freckled, Mick Brewer was tall and lean with straight dark hair. His coloring and facial features hinted at a Native American heritage.

"Brothers?" Zach repeated.

Zach took the words from her mouth.

"We're half brothers," Mick said. "I'm older."

"By a year is all," Benjie returned.

Zach's eyes rounded as he looked between the boys. He hadn't missed the irony, Emma noted. They were as different as he and Steve were.

"Can you ride, Mick?" Zach asked.

Benjie blew a loud raspberry.

"I asked Mick," Zach said drily.

Benjie's eyes popped wide at Zach's tone and he inched back.

"'Course I can ride." Mick swelled up his chest

and got in his brother's face. "Better than this little runt can."

"Naw, that's not true," Benjie defended himself. "You're the one who rides like a scaredy-cat."

"Do not."

"Do, too."

"Stop."

All heads turned to Zach as the thunderous words echoed throughout the stables. He held up a large gloved hand. "First rule. Less talking. And there is zero tolerance for name-calling."

"But..." Benjie said.

"Yes, sir, is the appropriate response," Zach said, his voice low and nearly a growl.

Emma's eyes rounded at the menacing tone in his voice.

Benjie blinked and swallowed. Then he inched back several paces. "Yes, sir."

"Mick, do you have a horse?" Zach asked.

"Yes, sir. We're all assigned horses to ride and groom."

"Then I'll trust you both to saddle up and wait outside." He looked between them. "Quietly."

"Yes, sir," both boys repeated, eager to leave.

"Helmets," Emma called after them.

"Yes, sir," Mick said.

Emma laughed. "I'm ma'am."

When she turned back to Zach, he pulled off his ball cap and then slapped it back on. His lips were twitching and his eyes sparkled with a humor she hadn't seen in years.

"That was impressive," Emma said as she grabbed her gloves and moved past Zach.

"Maybe I did get something out of the navy after all." He turned to her. "You going to be using the round pen?" he asked.

"Go ahead. I'll grab a fresh horse and take Benjie on a short trail ride and wear him out."

"Thanks."

"Don't thank me just yet." She lowered her voice. "You should know that Mick is one of our more difficult kids. He wears an attitude most of the time. When it comes to lessons, well, he's nervous in the saddle. Then he freezes up, gets defensive and can't hear a word you're telling him."

"And the horse?"

"We put him on Grace. My girls could ride Grace if I let them, but Mick hasn't mastered proper saddling, much less riding."

"How long has he been taking lessons?"

"Not long. He and Benjie arrived at the ranch at the end of the summer. City boys, in and out of foster homes."

"Thanks for the heads-up."

"No problem." She gave his leg a fleeting glance as she headed to another stall.

"My knee is fine," he called.

"*Fine* is a relative word," she mumbled to herself. Stubborn and prideful man. He wouldn't admit he was in pain and he refused to discuss the injury. Maybe Dutch could make some headway. The old cowboy had a silver tongue and a gift for weaseling information.

An hour later, with Benjie's lesson completed, Emma instructed the boy to head in to groom his horse before dinner. She led her own mare to the pen fence to observe Zach and Mick.

Mick finished adjusting the stirrups and turned to Zach, who stood several feet away, allowing the horse and rider to bond. "Done," Mick called.

Zach approached and circled Grace, carefully checking all aspects of the tack job the young rider had completed.

"Nice job, Mick," Zach said. "You groomed the horse, and the saddle is in place. Looks to me like you really know what you're doing."

Mick beamed for a moment then he stole a peek at his wristwatch. A frown darkened his face. "It took us so long."

"Are we in a rush?"

Mick shrugged his thin shoulders. "I guess not."

"This is not about clock watching, it is about learning how to do the job correctly. Grace's life and yours depend on it."

"Okay."

"Yes, sir," Zach corrected.

"Yes, sir."

"Give Grace a nice soft rub on her nose and talk to her, real quiet."

"I already did that."

"Can't ever give an animal too much loving. You're building a long-term relationship here."

Emma smiled at the words. He was so right. Zach might have spent the last twelve years in the navy, but he still remembered his cowboy roots.

Moments later, Zach nodded and gave Mick a thumbs-up. "You're ready to get on the horse."

Mick swallowed and his face paled. "But what if she bucks me?"

"Grace is your friend. Give her a chance. You trust her, right?"

He chewed his lip in thought before answering. "Maybe. But what if I fall off while I'm trying to get on?"

Zach raised his hands and stepped closer. "I'm right here. I'll catch you." He met Mick's worried gaze. "You're just going to sit in the saddle today. That's all. Nothing to it."

Mick didn't appear comforted by the words.

"Do I look like I can catch you?" Zach asked.

"Yes, sir, but I don't want to look stupid." Mick frowned yet again, this time with a glance over at Emma.

"I hear you." Zach pivoted around on his boot and narrowed his eyes. "Would you please excuse us, Miss Emma?"

"Oh, sure. Yes. Of course. Sorry." Embarrassed,

she turned away with the mare and headed inside to untack the horse.

Ten minutes later, the clop, clop of a horse plodding along on the stable floor had her peeking over the stall gate.

Zach offered a nod of acknowledgment as he and Grace walked down to the last stall on the left.

Emma took a deep breath. "I'm sorry for interrupting your lesson."

"No problem. You know how it is. He's a kid and he's terrified he'll humiliate himself in front of a beautiful woman."

"Beautiful woman?" she murmured.

"Look in the mirror lately?"

"I..." She cleared her throat and concentrated on the smooth velvet coat of the horse. "Well, yes, but usually what I see is the mother of twins."

"Look again."

"So how did you do?" she asked, letting the comment sail past her for analysis at a later time.

"Are you going to harass me about my knee again?"

When her hand slipped midstroke and the brush clattered to the ground, the chestnut mare snuffled an objection. "I'm talking about Mick," she clarified.

Minutes passed without a response.

Emma peeked over the stall, but couldn't see Zach. "Come on. Aren't you going to share?"

"I didn't realize you were waiting for a report," he called.

"Mick's been challenging since he arrived and I've had a few therapy sessions with him. Naturally, I'm curious."

"The lesson went well. Mick will be riding in no time."

"Really?"

"Yeah. I'm going to talk to Travis about taking over his lessons."

"So what did you do?"

"Can't say I did anything new. Went slow and acknowledged his fear. You're the therapist, you know the drill."

"Yes, but what did you do that Travis didn't?"

"Probably nothing. Maybe I got through to him because I can relate to this kid."

"Oh?" Emma cleaned off the brush and currycomb in her hand and gave the horse a pat to let him know they were done.

"Yeah. You might say we have a lot in common."

"Might?" She patted the horse again, checked the water and feed before latching the stall behind her.

"Yeah, might."

"Because both of you are big brothers with a chip on your shoulder, you mean?"

She thought she heard a chuckle but couldn't be sure.

"Something like that," he said.

Emma put the equipment away in the tack room across from Grace's stall. When she came out, Zach was waiting for her. He'd leaned back against Grace's stall gate with his weight on his right leg. "So tell me how this works."

"How what works?" she asked.

"The setup with the kids at the ranch."

Emma pulled her car keys from her back pocket and paused. "What do you want to know?"

"How the ranch helps the kids. What do you do that's so special?"

"What we do isn't special. It's simple and consistent. We create a new normal for them at Big Heart Ranch. We have two ranches here, the boys' ranch and the girls' ranch, separated by a road. The children are placed in a real house with house parents, not a dormitory. It's not a biological family, but it is a family of the heart. Their forever family from that point on. They have daily devotionals, lessons, homework, chores and all, like any other kid."

"That's it?"

"Zach, that's more than most of these kids have ever had. Every one of them comes from a situation that includes neglect and abuse. Many are orphaned or abandoned."

Zach took a deep breath at her words.

"When their heads hit the pillow at night, they no longer have the burden of worry or fear on their shoulders. We replace that with unconditional love and God's healing grace. We promise them that we will never lie to them and that we will always protect them. In return, they follow the ranch rules." She shrugged. "We free them to be children." Emma sighed. "Being a kid is highly undervalued these days."

For a long moment, Zach stared ahead as though unseeing. He was somewhere else, and she wished with all her heart that she understood where.

"Zach," she murmured. "You okay?"

He turned slightly and met her gaze. "Never better."

"Then I guess I'll see you later. I've got to get home to the girls."

"Thanks, Emma."

"For what?"

"For letting me work with Mick."

"Sure." Emma walked slowly to her car, puzzling over the conversation with Zach. She was certain that something remarkable had just happened but what that was eluded her.

Had she spoken to the Lord about Zach lately, or had she relegated him to a forgotten place in her prayers because she was annoyed by his dismissal of RangePro? His dismissal of her. It was time to remember her words about unconditional love and give Zach Norman what he deserved.

* * *

Zach's assessing gaze took in the Big Heart Ranch bunkhouse that would be his home for the next eight weeks. Though Spartan, the place had everything he needed. Small kitchenette and a little living room, complete with a love seat and recliner facing a television. Grabbing his duffel from the floor, he tossed it and his security badge from human resources onto one of the four empty beds.

Easing down onto the mattress, he closed his eyes a moment.

He was in pain.

Emma was right, and it totally grated.

His knee ached after a long day and he wasn't sure which hurt most, the smooth dismount while roping the mechanical bull or the multiple awkward exits from the saddle while working in the pasture. There was definitely a learning curve to remembering to guard the knee. Should have worn his brace.

Except, he hated the brace. Sure, it was worn under his jeans but he felt like everyone knew it was there.

He also refused to take the narcotics or the muscle relaxers that the physician ordered. Instead, Zach grabbed the familiar tube of prescription analgesic cream from his bag.

With a dab of cream in his hand, Zach rolled up the pant leg of his sweats and massaged the scars with vengeance. Six months ago, after the last unsuccessful surgery, he had come face-to-face with his future. Like the ranch kids, he was exploring his new normal.

In his last covert reconnaissance operation, Zach not only lost his best friend, Ian Clark, but his career and life as he'd known it for twelve years had been buried.

No matter how many surgeries he endured, he would never be 100 percent fit for duty again. The military docs were big on reminding him that he was fortunate to be alive, much less walk.

Lately, he was feeling far from grateful. What would he say to Ian's family when he visited them?

Sorry I made it and Ian didn't?

No, that wasn't going to cut it for parents with only one child, a child who was not coming home.

Zach hung his head.

He'd postponed meeting with the Clarks multiple times, waiting until he could figure that out. In the meantime, life as he knew it was over. A washed-up navy SEAL. Who was Zach Norman outside of the uniform? He didn't know, but he was about to find out.

As if on cue, the bunkhouse door flew open and Dutch Stevens, the wrangler Zach met earlier in the day, strode into the room, his scuffed boots beating a rhythm on the oak floorboards. The wizened cowboy tipped back his well-worn Western hat and pointedly stared at Zach's knee.

"That's quite a few scars you got there."

"A road map to the unknown after three surgeries."

"Ouch." Dutch grimaced.

"It looks worse than it is."

"Not from where I stand, so I guess I'll have to take your word for that." Dutch shook his head. "Did you meet Tripp Walker, the equine manager?"

"Yeah. Talkative guy."

Dutch chuckled. "Tripp believes that if more people would think before they spoke, they'd open their mouth a whole lot less."

"He's on to something."

"Not sure I agree with him. But that's our Tripp." He rubbed his chin and kept talking. "Anyhow, he's got weights and a bench set up for the staff in the back of the equipment barn near Travis's office. Use them anytime you like."

"Thanks, Dutch."

"You looked pretty good out there roping with Travis. Like maybe you've done that before."

"A time or two," Zach admitted. "Did a little bulldogging in my time, as well as heading and heeling."

"You don't say?" The words held a tinge of awed respect. "A real cowboy then. I suspected as much."

"My father used to run a ranch outside of Pawhuska. That's how I met the Maxwell kids.

When they were pulled out of foster care by a relative, they lived right next door."

Dutch gave a slow nod. "Sure. That's right. Jay Norman. Retired a few years ago. Steve was your brother?"

"Half brother."

"Sorry for your loss."

"Thanks."

"I was out of town during the funeral. I guess I missed meeting you then."

Zach nodded. He'd been in and out on the day of the funeral. Arrived on the red-eye and left before sunset.

"Shame for Emma and those babies. She and Steve weren't married very long, either."

"No, I guess not."

"I know she's glad to have Steve's family here."

"Maybe so," Zach murmured.

"You're gonna need linens if you're staying." Dutch walked over to a closet and pulled open the door. "They're in here."

"Thanks, but who said I'm staying?" Zach asked.

"Aw, don't worry. Travis said to zip my lips. I can do that on occasion."

"I appreciate it. So where do you bunk?" Zach asked.

"Over yonder." He raised a thumb. "Couple of bunkhouses to the right. This here is the guest bunkhouse."

"I'm the only guest?"

"For the moment." Dutch gave a nod, obviously still thinking and sizing up Zach.

"So you grew up with the Maxwells?" Dutch continued.

"I did." Zach smiled as he recalled the first time he saw Emma. Five years old, with long dark braids, a big grin, full of sass and already riding. He hadn't thought about that in a long time.

"Must have been pretty young, huh?" Dutch said.

"Too young. No one should have to deal with the death of their parents and then have their foundation ripped out from under them like they did."

"Yet, that's exactly what our kids here on Big Heart Ranch deal with. All of them."

Zach paused. "I hadn't thought of it like that."

"Sure enough. That's what has made Lucy, Travis and Emma so determined to turn around the burden of their past. They took the land their mother's cousin left them in Timber and started this ranch. A new beginning." He shook his head. "Those three bring good to everything they touch."

"I believe that." Zach put the cover back on the jar and tightened the lid. "How long have you been on Big Heart Ranch, Dutch?"

"Oh, a while and a half, for sure."

"That long, huh?"

Hand on the doorknob, Dutch hesitated before he headed out. "You know, I was just like you, once upon a time. Came for a visit and ended up staying."

Zach blinked at the bold statement. "I'm not staying. This is only temporary."

"Oh?" The old cowboy stared him down. "Just sticking around until you finish mending?"

"My knee, you mean?"

He shook his head and offered a sly smile. "Don't take offense, but I got a feeling the good Lord put you in the path of Big Heart Ranch for a reason and it's got nothing to do with your knee." Dutch tapped his own chest and placed a hand over his heart as his gaze met Zach's.

Zach narrowed his eyes. "Though that isn't my plan, I wouldn't rule out the possibility."

A grin lit up Dutch's face, and he offered a nod of respect. "I expected an argument."

"Not from me. I've learned to never say *never.* Life has tossed me into too many situations where my next move was completely a walk of faith."

"Wise man," Dutch murmured.

"I don't know about that. Not so much wisdom as it is lots of experience making mistakes." He rolled down the leg of his sweatpants. "Where's that meeting I'm supposed to go to tonight?"

"Meeting? It's a party. One of the biggest of the year."

"Okay, where's this mandatory fun I'm required to attend?"

"Downtown Timber. Oklahoma Rose restaurant. Across from the Timber General Store. There's a parking lot behind the restaurant. Might make it easier on your leg."

"Thanks."

The door closed softly and Zach pulled out a bandanna to wipe his hands while thinking about his conversation with the wrangler.

Easier. He wasn't handicapped. It was a simple knee injury. So he couldn't jump out of planes anymore. That wasn't a good enough reason for the world to keep trying to turn him into a desk jockey.

Zach paused. Unless they were right. If so, he wouldn't be much use to Travis on the ranch either, would he?

Once again, the urge to leave rose up strong. What was he doing here anyhow? Had the Lord led him here or had he come to Oklahoma simply to clear his conscience?

Twice he had changed his mind during the long drive from California. The only thing that kept him from making a U-turn on I-40 eastbound was the promise made to Ian's folks. He was determined to keep that promise. Their son was gone and they needed closure only Zach could provide. He was willing to relive the anguish of that mission to do that.

Besides, where would he go? He didn't have a home anymore. His apartment in California had been cleared out and his few possessions put into storage until January.

Zach took a ragged breath and ran a hand through his hair. His gaze landed on last year's photo Christmas card Emma had sent him that peeked out of his duffel. Elizabeth and Rachel.

His brother's children. Family. They deserved so much more from him. He owed Emma and Steve that. In truth, he was long overdue for facing the past. It was time to man up. Maybe if he did he'd find the path to his future, however uncertain that future might be.

Chapter Three

"Candy canes?" Emma asked.

Lucy Maxwell Harris held up the plastic shopping bag that dangled from her right arm. "Check."

Emma pulled open the door of the restaurant for her sister, who waddled past and headed into the Oklahoma Rose with a protective hand on her large abdomen.

"Whew." Lucy ran a hand through her dark cap of hair and adjusted the Santa hat on her head. "Is it hot in here?"

"No. The female air-conditioning system is a little overworked during pregnancy."

"Is that it?"

Emma nodded. "Any success finding mistletoe?"

"Got that, too. I bought extra to take home to Jack."

"Isn't Jack coming?" Emma asked.

"I wish. He's in charge of the papier mâché volcano the kids are making for the science fair."

"Hmm." Emma shook her head. "Difficult to say who got the better assignment."

Lucy sniffed appreciatively and glanced around. "Oh, this place smells wonderful. Is that steak? You know, I haven't had anything to eat in over an hour."

A hand to her mouth, Emma stifled a chuckle while grabbing a menu from a nearby empty table. "Here you go. We won't let you starve. I promise."

"They have sweet potato fries." She shot Emma a conspiratorial glance. "Do not tell Jack, but it's apparent that I got the better deal tonight."

"May I help you?" the smiling hostess asked.

"Big Heart Ranch Christmas party," Emma said. "I was here this morning. The manager said you could unlock the room for us."

"Christmas? And here I thought that was a typo," the woman murmured.

"We like to get a jump on the holidays at Big Heart."

"I guess so. Do you want to schedule Groundhog Day now, as well?"

Emma choked on a laugh. "I'll get back to you on that."

They followed the woman through the restaurant, weaving past tables toward a banquet room.

As they passed the small dance area where a band was setting up, Emma nudged her sister.

"Look. Live music tonight," she said.

"Those are the Dixie Hens," the hostess said, excitement lacing her voice. "They're almost famous around these parts. Last year they went on tour with L.C. Kestner."

"Who?" Lucy mouthed to Emma.

Emma shrugged and rolled her eyes.

"I'm happy to ask the band to play Christmas dance tunes for your group," the woman continued.

"Thank you. That would be great," Emma said.

"Planning to dance?" Lucy asked.

"Perhaps. I am, after all, highly skilled at the hokey-pokey. Ask my daughters."

Lucy grinned as the hostess unlocked the door to a private room. Taking a step in, she paused to look up at the ceiling where glittering snowflakes suspended on clear fishing line gently swayed.

"Emma, this is beautiful."

Emma peeked over her sister's shoulder at the long tables covered with red tablecloths. Burlap runners decorated the center of the tables and were dotted with mason jars tied with red and green ribbons and filled with berried greenery. In the corner of the room, an artificial Christmas tree complete with ornaments and twinkling colored lights stood proudly. Red and green envelopes with the staff's holiday stipends tucked inside also hung from the branches.

"I love Christmas." Emma sighed with pleasure and inspected the room once again. "It did turn out nice, didn't it?"

"Come on, Em. Nice? This is perfect. Rustic and Christmassy. This is the perfect way to launch the Holiday Roundup."

"That's what I thought, too."

"What's in those shiny silver favor boxes next to each place setting?"

"My secret recipe truffles to take home."

Lucy did a double take. "You're amazing. When did you have time to decorate if you were baking?"

"I snuck over here this afternoon after the cutout cookies were done."

"Of course you did. I forget that you inherited the family gene for OCS."

"What?"

"Overcommitted syndrome. Emma, do you ever relax?"

"Sometimes." Relaxing only gave her time to think. She didn't need more time to think than she already had.

"Try to remember the *D* word that Jack taught me when he hired Iris as my admin."

"*D* word?"

"Delegate, Em. Delegate."

"Delegate, huh? That certainly sounds odd coming from the queen of micromanaging."

"Be nice. I'm still a work in progress." She glanced at Emma. "What happened to your admin?"

"It turned out she was allergic to the ranch. I'll get around to hiring a new one, soon enough," Emma said. "So did you bring your gift to trade?"

Lucy gasped. "The gift exchange!"

Emma reached into her tote bag and handed Lucy a wrapped box. "No worries. I brought several in case someone forgot theirs."

"Okay, this time your OCS saved the day. What's inside?"

"I can't tell you. That spoils the fun of the exchange."

"Ow," Lucy moaned. "Junior just kicked me." She placed one hand on her belly and one on her lower back.

"How are you feeling, Luce?"

"Large." She sighed. "And don't you dare laugh."

"Trust me, you are not large. Not like I was, expecting twins."

"Tell that to my lower back. And my feet are so swollen that I can't wear my red cowboy boots." She grimaced. "Aren't you glad you asked?"

"Think positive. You're having a Christmas baby."

"I am thinking positive. I'm positive that my back is killing me."

"Turn around."

Lucy obliged and Emma massaged her sister's lower back with the heel of her hand.

"Bliss," Lucy murmured. "Oh, look, our staff are arriving."

The band began to play an upbeat and popular Christmas tune at the same time the front door of the restaurant opened and the party guests began to pour in to the small foyer. The scene seemed straight out of a holiday movie. Everyone was smiling, laughing and carrying gaily wrapped presents. Snow falling outside would have made things complete, but the November weather continued to be unseasonably warm.

"Look," Lucy said. "Dutch is already on the dance floor."

"It's hard to resist a rousing chorus of 'Frosty the Snowman.'"

Shivers swept through Emma and she immediately turned her attention back to the front door of the restaurant. Zach had arrived. He wore a nondescript gray dress shirt and charcoal slacks. Nondescript on anyone but Zach.

"Zach is here," Lucy commented.

"I see him," Emma murmured. She swallowed and put a hand to her chest where her heart beat wildly.

Lucy tilted her head and blatantly stared at the

tall former navy SEAL. "Why was it you fell for Steve instead of Zach?"

For a brief second the answer stumped Emma. Then she remembered. Steve had courted her. Zach had never made a single overture beyond friendship. She'd fallen for the Norman brother who'd first loved her.

"I've always preferred my life simple," Emma said aloud. "Zach is anything but simple."

"He's simply handsome." Lucy sighed.

"Definitely hard to ignore," Emma admitted.

"Yes. Which would be why every woman in the restaurant is checking him out," Lucy said.

"The man is completely oblivious."

Lucy grinned. "Just like my Jack. I like that in a man."

Emma laughed. "You're incorrigible, Lucy."

"Do you ever think about dating, Em?"

"Women with small children don't have time to date. What is dating anyhow? It's auditioning husbands. I'm not looking for another husband."

"That's not all it is. It can be cultivating a friendship with someone with the same interests as you."

"I don't have time to cultivate anything but dirty laundry and mold in my refrigerator."

"While I can relate to that, I'm guessing your house is spotless."

"All the same, the last thing I need is a man in

my life. I'm not ready for that kind of challenge. I may never be ready."

"Zach was always your friend. You could do worse than Zach Norman in your life in any capacity."

Emma's hand froze. "What are you talking about?"

"I'm just saying."

"Well, don't. Zach is like a brother to me." She silently corrected herself. He was never a brother to her. A best friend? Yes. Though that bond had disappeared once she married Steve. She had struggled many times over the past few years trying to figure out why they couldn't at least be friends.

"Zach? Like your brother?" Lucy echoed Emma's words. "Um, not exactly." She turned and met Emma's gaze, then released a small gasp. "You're afraid."

Emma glanced away and didn't answer her sister.

"Em," she said softly. "Steve died in a car accident. Three years ago. You're entitled to grieve in your own way and in your own time, but please, don't let fear get a foothold in your life."

"I won't have the rug pulled out from under me again. I might not survive the next time."

"There are no guarantees for any of us, Emma.

You and Travis and I know that firsthand. In fact, every child on Big Heart Ranch knows that lesson."

"Lucy," Emma warned.

The eldest Maxwell sibling was silent for a long moment staring across the restaurant at Zach. "Do you ever wonder why Zach has stayed away?"

"I assumed it was something between him and Steve. I've asked. The man circles any sort of substantial answer with vague responses."

"You have eight weeks to find out what's going on in that navy SEAL head of his."

"Eight weeks?" Emma's hand shot to her lips, setting the decorative red and green sleigh bells on her bracelet into tinkling motion. "What are you talking about?"

"He's here until January."

"Says who?"

"Me. I signed off on his HR paperwork this morning."

"I'm confused. Why would Zach have paperwork with Big Heart Ranch?"

"Travis hired him."

Emma's jaw dropped. "Zach?"

"Yes. He picked up his security badge this morning."

"Why would Zach…? Why would Travis…?" she sputtered.

"Uh-oh. Don't look now, but Mr. Navy SEAL has his eye on you," Lucy said.

"What?" She turned toward the door.

"He's sort of lost out there in the crowd. Go save him," Lucy said quietly.

Emma blew a soft raspberry. "Zach Norman does not need saving."

"Everyone needs saving, Emma."

"Fine. Whatever." She started across the room, pausing at intervals to greet the staff.

Zach's gaze followed her the entire time.

"I heard you're staying until January," she said when she was finally standing in front of him, looking up at all six feet five inches of solid muscle.

Zach offered a silent scrutiny, his expression shuttered.

"Well?" she prompted.

"Hi to you, too, Emma." He nodded and stared at her. "Blinking reindeer earrings, huh?" His gaze moved to assess her holiday party outfit. "Interesting sweater."

She glanced down at the knit vest with the ornament embellishments. "Ugly sweater contest."

"I'm guessing you're going to win."

When Zach winked, Emma's eyes widened with surprise.

Focus, Emma.

She pushed the hair back from her face, setting

her jingle bell bracelet into motion. The sound was a welcome distraction.

"Nice bracelet," he said.

She began to smile and then remembered that she was annoyed. The man had bested her. Again.

"So is it true? Are you staying?" she asked.

"Who told you?"

"The source is really not important."

"I'm working for Travis."

"You are so stubborn. You'll work for Travis, though your knee says otherwise, but you refuse to even discuss RangePro."

When Zach just stared at her, Emma almost backed down from the stormy gaze. Instead, she stood her ground and refused to look away.

"Could we call a truce on this whole RangePro thing? At least until the holidays are over?" he finally said. "I mean, isn't this time of year supposed to reflect peace on earth? Goodwill to all men?" Zach paused. "Even me?"

Emma wilted at his quote from the Bible. Suddenly, she recalled the kid next door forced to return home to an apathetic mother for the holidays when he longed to stay at his father's ranch for Christmas.

Ashamed of herself, she took a deep breath. Why was it the man brought out the cranky and uncharitable in her?

Big Heart Ranch staff continued to enter the

restaurant, pushing Emma closer to Zach as they tried to make their way to the banquet room.

Emma stepped back, struggling to overcome with a smiling face and a positive attitude. "You're right. I apologize."

"A holiday truce, then?"

When Zach held out a hand, she nodded and stared at his hand, afraid to actually touch him. "A truce it is. The party is this way." She started toward the back of the restaurant.

"Excuse me, Emma," a woman said from behind her.

She turned. "Oh, Zach, this is Josee. One of our wranglers."

"Pleased to meet you, ma'am."

"Zach, is it?" the pretty blond-haired woman asked.

"Yes, ma'am."

"Would you like to dance?"

"Pardon me?" Zach's eyes widened as his gaze skimmed the dance floor.

"I wondered if you'd like to dance," Josee repeated.

"I'm so sorry, ma'am. I already promised this dance to Emma."

"Another time, then." Josee smiled and looked from Zach to Emma with curiosity before she turned away.

"You didn't promise me this dance."

"I fully intended to." Laughter filled his gray

eyes. “Besides, isn’t this your favorite song?” he asked.

Emma cocked her head. “That’s ‘Jingle Bell Rock.’”

He held out his hand. The hand she’d avoided only minutes before.

“As if you really want to dance,” Emma mumbled.

“Are you going to turn me down in front of all these people?”

Emma glanced around at the speculative gazes turned their way. He had her and he knew it.

Leaving her no choice, Zach took her hand. “It’s a two-step,” he said. “Your other hand goes to my shoulder and then you step.”

“I know how to dance.” She hesitantly placed her left hand on his shoulder. “What about your knee?”

“Let me worry about my knee.”

“But…”

Zach shook his head. “You’re a substitute mother to sixty some kids at Big Heart Ranch. That’s plenty, don’t you think? Besides, I don’t need a momma.”

“I… I…” *What was he saying?* Didn’t he realize that she could not concentrate on the conversation while her hand was enveloped in his?

A long silence stretched between them as Emma worked hard not to tangle her feet and fall on her face.

When Lucy walked past the dance floor and her gaze connected with Emma's, her sister stopped and did a double take.

"Lucy sure looks, um, ripe," Zach said. "When's she due?"

"Christmas."

"*Christmas*. Everything seems to revolve around Christmas."

"Only for eight weeks of the year."

"Only eight weeks," he murmured.

Emma turned her head and stared at her hand in his. His hand was so large, yet hers seemed to fit perfectly.

"This is quite the crowd," he observed.

"This is nothing. Wait until Thanksgiving."

"Was I supposed to bring a present?" Zach asked with a nod toward the guests who walked past with gifts tucked under their arms.

"They're fun white elephant exchanges. I brought extras."

He glanced toward the banquet room filling up with people. "Tell me about this Christmas party."

She shrugged. "It's a party. Eat food, make merry. Mingle."

"I don't—"

"Mingle," she finished for him. "Somehow I thought you might say that." Emma sighed. "But you know Dutch and Tripp and Travis. Chat with them."

"Travis has his wife." He raised his brows. "And it looks like they found the mistletoe."

She turned in Zach's arms to see Travis kissing his new bride beneath the mistletoe that he had hung in the doorway of the banquet room.

"Young love," Emma said. "You know how it is."

"Can't say that I do." He glanced around. "Looks like the single men are outnumbered around here."

"That's true. Tonight it's just you, Tripp and Dutch."

"No dates invited?"

"Dutch's sweetheart is the ranch physician, General Rue Butterfield. Rue is out of town at the moment with a family emergency."

"And Tripp? What's his story?"

"Tripp? Oh, he'd never bring a date. He's even more private than you are."

"Am I private?"

"As locked up as a clam. If you want to pass the time, ask Dutch to tell you about the John Wayne impersonator he saw in Tulsa last week. By the time he finishes with his tall tale, dinner will be served, then we'll get down to business."

"What business is that?"

"The Holiday Roundup."

The song ended and Emma stepped away from him, wrapping her arms around herself. Relief and disappointment crowded her at the same time.

"The Holiday Roundup," he repeated. Zach rubbed a hand over his jaw. "It seems apparent that I showed up at Big Heart Ranch at the wrong time of year."

"Or maybe it's the right time, and you just don't know it yet."

When his dark eyes met hers, Emma's heart stopped and everything seemed to be in slow motion as the words she had just uttered echoed through her while Zach Norman turned away.

Maybe it was the right time, and she just didn't know it yet.

Zach downed his eggnog and turned to Dutch. "We're doing what?"

Around them, holiday music continued to play as the party wound down. The old wrangler had just dashed his high hopes of slipping out of the party soon. Zach was certain he had a rash over most of him from being social tonight. He didn't do social, and yet here he was.

Dutch grabbed the last broken cookies from a tray that only a few hours ago overflowed with Christmas cutout cookies and popped them into his mouth with a loud smack of his lips. "I'm telling you, Miss Emma makes the best cookies. Her chocolate muffins would take a blue ribbon anywhere."

"Dutch, quit eating and answer me."

"I told you. It's chore-pickin' time." He nodded to the large box wrapped like a Christmas package that sat at the end of the banquet table.

"Miss Lucy and Miss Emma divide up the chores for the Holiday Roundup and you pick yours from that big box there. Everyone gets two."

"I never heard of anything so unorganized. This is worse than being voluntarily told in the navy."

"The gals say it keeps the program fresh. New ideas and perspectives and everyone owns the event."

Zach released a breath. "I can guarantee there is nothing that resembles my skill set in that box."

"Don't matter. It's the spirit of the season that counts. Making memories. Having fun." Dutch's gaze scanned the room. "Did I ever tell you how I was Mary in the living nativity one year?"

"Now you're messing with me."

The seasoned cowboy offered a slow shake of his head. "Wish I was. I had to shave my 'stache."

Zach ran a hand over his face and swallowed.

"Come on." Dutch nodded to the box. "Best get it over with."

"You first," Zach said as he followed.

Dutch put a hand in the box, pulled out two papers and stepped aside to allow Zach to do the same. "What did you get?" Dutch asked a moment later.

"I haven't opened them yet," Zach returned.

"I'll trade you. Sight unseen."

"Not a chance." Zach gave a nod toward Dutch's slips of paper. "What did you get?"

The cowboy grimaced. "Porta potty duty and horse-drawn carriage driver."

"That doesn't sound too bad."

"Depends on which direction the wind is blowing."

Zach stared at the seemingly innocuous papers in his own hand.

"Hurry up and open yours," Dutch said. "Miss Emma's coming around with her clipboard to document your assignment."

"Then I better get moving."

It would be a very good idea to keep his distance from both clipboards and the youngest Maxwell sibling. He was still trying to figure out what got into him earlier. Dancing with Emma. That came out of nowhere.

He was beginning to realize that if he wasn't on guard at all times, history would be repeated. His history…of acting like a love-struck idiot when Emma was nearby.

Dodging around the buffet table, Zach headed to the other side of the room. He stooped behind greenery to examine the Christmas tree decorations, though his height made it nearly impossible to hide.

"Your envelope is near the back of the tree."

She found him.

"I wasn't looking for an envelope."

"What were you doing?"

He raised a hand and decided against explaining. "How did anyone know to give me an envelope?"

"That's a very good question," Emma said. "Lucy's admin, Iris, reads minds. You can thank her later." Emma plucked a green envelope from the tree and handed it to him.

Zach shook his head. "This is really not necessary."

"Deal with it. It's a Christmas present."

"Presents are for little kids."

She scoffed. "Who told you that?"

My mother when I turned six and my parents divorced.

"It was understood at my home."

"Oh, Zach, I'm so sorry. While the holidays aren't simply about presents, certainly a child should experience the joy of giving and receiving."

"It's really a moot point, Emma. I don't do Christmas."

"You don't believe in Christmas?" She offered a dramatic sigh. "Sort of makes you like Scrooge, doesn't it?"

"Does that make you Tiny Tim?"

She cocked her head in thought. "I'd like to think of myself as one of the benevolent characters who show you the error of your ways."

"Right. Right." He stared at her ridiculous blinking reindeers. "For the record, I never said I don't believe in Christmas."

"Could you elaborate then? What is it about Christmas that you have a problem with? I mean besides presents and Christmas parties. And by the way, I don't know if you've noticed but you sure have a long list of things that you have issues with."

"Emma, you're sort of an overanalyzer. Anybody ever mention that?"

Her eyes rounded. "You have issues with me, too?"

"Now you're putting words in my mouth."

"I'm a therapist. I analyze. It comes with the territory."

"You're a child therapist and I'm not a child."

Emma shrugged. "The same principles apply to grown-up children."

"You aren't *my* therapist."

Her lips formed a thin line, and Zach could practically see the steam coming out of her ears.

"What are you thinking?" he asked.

"You don't want to know."

"I asked, didn't I?"

"I'm trying to figure out what happened to make you so disillusioned. And why does it seem like you're angry with me? We used to be friends."

"That was a long time ago. We were kids."

She jerked back as though she'd been slapped.

Zach immediately regretted opening his big mouth. Emma was everything good and right in the world, and he had managed to dim her light with his special brand of darkness.

"May I see your assignment slips?" The words were clipped and flat.

"Sure."

He pulled the crumpled papers from his pocket, smoothed them out and glanced at the words. What harm could come from putting up lights and greenery?

"Oh." She released a long-suffering sigh.

"Oh?"

"You're on my team."

"I'm sorry," he said.

"There's no need to apologize."

"Sure feels like I ought to." He shrugged. "So where do I start?"

"Excuse me, Emma, Zach. I hate to interrupt."

Both Zach and Emma turned to find Lucy standing close with a concerned expression.

"What's wrong?" Emma asked her sister.

"I've maxed out. I'm so sorry, but I'm going to have to bail on you."

"Do you need a ride home?" Zach asked.

"Oh, how sweet of you to offer, but Travis and AJ are dropping me off. They live right down the road." She glanced around at the room and frowned before she put a hand on Emma's arm. "I feel horrible leaving you with cleanup."

"Go, Lucy," Emma said.

"Are you sure?"

"Cleanup is my specialty. You of all people know how true that is."

"I'll help," Zach said. The words slipped from his mouth before he had a chance to outrun them.

Lucy and Emma turned to him, startled expressions on their faces.

He offered an embarrassed chuckle. "Come on. I think I can handle a little disaster recovery, ladies."

Emma bit her lip, saying nothing.

When Lucy stood on tiptoes from her five-foot-two-inch height and planted a kiss on his cheek, Zach froze.

"What was that for?" he murmured.

"Just to say thank you." She offered him and Emma a benevolent smile. "Take good care of my sister."

"Oh, good grief," Emma said. "Lucy, will you please go home?"

"I'm going."

"Call me in the morning to check in," Emma called after her. "And stay home if you need to."

"I just might."

"Good." Emma grabbed a trash bag.

"Let me help with that."

"Zach, you really don't need to stay," Emma said.

"I'm on your team."

"That's the Holiday Roundup."

"Let me help you get out of here and home to your children." He paused. "Besides, I just promised your sister..."

She crossed her arms and tapped her foot on the vinyl floor tiles. "Do I look like I need to be taken care of?"

Five foot four and 100 percent self-sufficient. That was Emma. Everyone leaned on her and she leaned on no one. Some things never changed. He bit back the retort on the end of his tongue. "A promise is a promise," he murmured.

"Okay, fine." She waved a hand in the air. "Start with the tree and be sure all the envelopes have been removed."

"What do you want to do with the tree?"

"My supplies are in that closet over there. Put a giant trash bag over the tree and tie the bag at the bottom. Then we'll stick the entire thing in my car."

When Emma grabbed a chair and stepped up on the seat to reach the hanging snowflakes, Zach considered suggesting that he tackle the ceiling, but decided that the better plan was to keep his mouth firmly shut. Instead, he kept a close eye on her while he bagged the tree and then started taking down the hanging lights on the back wall.

One by one, Emma removed each snowflake. She brushed the silver sparkles from her clothes and hair while she assessed the other decorations in the room.

Eyes on the mistletoe, she dragged the chair to the doorway and reached for the berried greenery. Her fingers barely skimmed the curling red ribbon tied to the stem.

"That Travis. No respect for short people," she muttered. With a soft grunt of frustration, Emma stretched toward the swaying bundle yet again, setting the bells from her bracelet into a cacophony of noise. The angle of the mistletoe still made it difficult to reach.

"I got it." Zach's hand touched hers when they reached for the mistletoe at the same time. When Emma swayed, about to fall, he acted on instinct. His hands spanned her waist as he caught her and set her on her feet on the floor. "You okay?"

She nodded, releasing silver sparkles that danced from her hair onto the smooth skin of her face.

Zach stepped away from the land mine situation and kept his hands firmly at his sides.

What had he gotten himself into?

Christmas couldn't arrive too soon because working with Emma was pretty much the single most hazardous duty he'd ever been called upon to do. Could he work alongside a woman he might very well still be in love with without getting his heart broken a second time?

One of the random sayings from SEAL training ran through his head and he realized he better hold the words close, because yeah, it was time to get comfortable being uncomfortable.

Chapter Four

Zach wiped the sweat from his brow and caught his breath after hiking up the steep stairs to the loft of the equipment barn. He adjusted his knee brace and stood straight. Towering stacks of plastic storage bins lined the entire far wall. Surely, not all of those bins were filled with holiday lights. Or were they?

A moment later, the door to the barn creaked open and the humming of a holiday tune reached his ears.

"Are you up there?" Emma's voice echoed into the rafters.

"Yes, Rudolph. I'm up here."

"Funny," she muttered.

Emma grunted as her boots hit each step. "Whose bright idea was it to store these up here last year? This stairwell is ridiculously steep and it sure could use a railing." Her dark head popped up onto the landing and she glanced around. “How did you get up here with your knee?”

“Slowly,” he said. “Give me your hand.”

“I’ve got it.”

“Stop arguing. Give me your hand.”

Emma blinked at his command. “Yes, sir. Take these bags first.”

“I smell coffee.”

“That’s because I brought coffee.” She lifted the bags in the air and Zach grabbed them.

“What’s in the other bag?”

“Chocolate muffins.”

Emma held out a hand and Zach hauled her into the loft. They stood inches from each other. He reluctantly released her hand and kept his eyes on the planked floor as his heart pounded loud enough for her to hear.

“Thank you.” In one dainty movement, she removed her hand from his and dusted off her Wranglers. “Here.” Emma handed the other bag to him.

Zach peeked inside at the muffins. “These are still warm.”

“Uh-huh. I made them this morning.”

He stared at her.

“What? Baking is therapeutic for me.”

“You may be the therapist, but my gut tells me that this is not normal.”

“Give your gut a muffin and tell it to stop complaining.”

“Hey, I’m not complaining. Merely observing.”

"Right." Emma pulled two plastic to-go cups from the other bag.

He glanced down at the coffees. "Which one is mine?"

"They're both cream only."

Zach narrowed his gaze. "How did you know I take cream?"

She shrugged. "Good memory."

"I guess so." He grabbed a muffin and took a bite, eyes widening. "Dutch was right. You're in the wrong business."

"Excuse me?"

"Why aren't you baking for a living?"

"I don't have time."

"Emma, I've been here five days, and already it's clear that you milk more minutes out of twenty-four hours than anyone else on this ranch."

"That may be true, but I can't be a therapist, a mother, a Big Heart Ranch Band-Aid, run Ranch-Pro and open a bakery."

"I can think of at least one thing on that career list that can go away."

"Me, too, but you refuse to help with Ranch-Pro."

He sighed. "And we were doing so well up to this point."

"That's because we haven't seen each other since Monday. Travis has had you knee deep in calves."

"I'm sorry I couldn't help you sooner."

She raised a hand. "It will all work out. It always does."

"Does it?" He cocked his head and looked at her.

"Sure. This is what life is all about. Unexpected blessings. Lucy's baby news, Travis's wedding and then the calves decide this is the time to make an appearance."

"You sure find a way to put a happy spin on everything."

"Why not?" She looked at him, back straight with indignation. "What's to be gained from being negative?"

Zach considered the question but didn't answer. When he was around Emma, he wasn't able to justify his rotten attitude. Her journey to today was no less difficult as his own. Yet, she remained an encouragement, and for the first time he considered rethinking his stance.

She took a swig of coffee and pulled out a clipboard. "Not all of these bins are for our team."

"Glad to hear that. Which ones do I need to take out of the loft?"

"The blue, red and green ones."

Zach blinked. "That's over half of them. What's inside the blue, red and green bins?"

"The blue bins are the lights. The red ones are outside ornaments and the green bins are velvet bows."

"There must be fifty bins of lights."

She tapped on the clipboard and fingered through several pages. "Fifty-two. Very close."

"What do you do with fifty-two bins of lights?"

"After you haul them down with the bale elevator, you plug them in and make sure they work."

"You're telling me we have to check every single string of lights in all these boxes?"

"Someone has to," Emma said.

"Yeah, they have companies that do this. Professionals."

"For a price."

"This is going to take a chunk of my life," he groused.

"You're a navy SEAL. Don't you get more done by noon than most people do all day?" She pulled out her phone. "It's only 7:00 a.m."

"That's the army."

"What do navy SEALs do?"

"Last time I checked we don't do redundant," he muttered. "Can we plug them in after we hang them?"

"No."

"Why not? Seems simple enough. Hang them and then replace the ones that aren't working."

"The cherry picker is rented by the hour."

"So it takes a little longer. In the end, it will save someone's sanity. Mine."

"Zach, we're a private charity. We get zero state or federal funding. Our administration consists of about five salaried staff. Then there are the wranglers, the house parents and various other part-time staff."

"Your point?"

"We don't hire out that which we can do ourselves."

"An Emma-ism?"

"Are you making fun of me?" She glared at him.

"Okay, sorry, that was a cheap shot, especially since you made muffins." He couldn't help but smile. This banter was like old times and he sort of liked it.

"Look, Zach, we check the lights first to save money on the cherry picker rental and we don't pay someone else to do the setup because that would defeat the purpose. We're all working together to create Christmas memories along with celebrating in the true spirit of the holiday."

Zach groaned. "Again with the spirit of the holiday."

"Okay, I'm serious this time. When *did* you become such a Scrooge?"

He flashed to the last miserable Christmas before he turned eighteen and left home. Without answering Emma, he lifted the lid of a bin and inspected the neatly wrapped bundles of green cord and lights. "Where did you get these lights?"

"I think they were donated."

"They're prehistoric."

"Vintage."

He fingered the strands. “How many lights are there?”

“I don’t know. Thousands?”

“More like millions. You do realize that LED string lights are far more energy efficient, right?”

“This is what we have. Deal with it.”

Deal with it? He had to give the woman credit. Even in a plaid Western shirt and Wranglers, Emma Maxwell managed to look all sweetness and sugar despite having the quick wit and sharp tongue that would have put his recruit-training navy chief to shame.

“What’s the plan for the lights?” he asked.

“We decorate every single tree along the main road through the boys’ ranch, including the gazebo and the stage we set up in front of the pond. The front gate, as well.”

Zach frowned. “All that? Seems to me that I do not have a complete understanding of the scope of this mission.”

“Mission?” She raised her brows. “What don’t you get about this mission, Sergeant Norman?”

Zach snorted at the title. “It’s Lieutenant Norman.”

“Your question, Lieutenant Norman?”

“Why all the lights?”

“We deliver the complete holiday experience here at Big Heart Ranch. Besides the living nativity, there’s live music at the gazebo and in front of the pond. The schedule alternates bell ringers, carolers and an ensemble of musicians from the ranch staff. Visitors may walk or take a horse-drawn carriage through a portion of the boys' ranch to enjoy the program. In addition, at the end of the route, we provide gingerbread and hot cider or hot coffee for our guests. Fair trade only."

"You sound like a travel ad."

"I have to talk to all the businesses in Timber and surrounding towns to get them to support the roundup. I can recite that spiel in my sleep."

"What do you charge?"

"It's free."

His head jerked back. "Free? How do you make any money?"

"The Timber community donates plenty to make this happen. Plus we have the Christmas trees."

"Christmas trees?"

"Yes. Lucy is in charge of the tree sales. She has an entire team rotating each day from noon to 7:00 p.m."

"I'm stunned."

"I don't see why. This is our fifth year and we've pulled it off every year without any major glitches."

"Maybe we could improve the process with the purchase of state-of-the-art lights."

"New lights are not in the budget. It would eat into our profit margin. The money from the tree sales goes toward gifts for the children of the

Pawhuska Children's Orphanage. Each family here at Big Heart Ranch adopts several children for the event and our families go out and buy the presents with the tree sales money. Think of it like an angel tree."

"Who buys presents for the children who live here at Big Heart Ranch?"

"Zach, the families on the ranch are like regular families out in the world. They have their own exchange, but we suggest one gift each. Christmas isn't about receiving, it's about giving. It's about the greatest gift giver of all. The present that came to us on Christmas morning."

Zach frowned.

"Now what?" Emma released an exasperated sigh.

"All this sounds great in theory, but in my experience, Christmas is hype."

"No, the world does hype. We don't do hype here at Big Heart Ranch, Zach. Wait. You'll see."

Her eyes sparkled with an excitement that might make even the most cynical believe. *Might.*

"What if it snows?" he asked.

"We're hoping for snow. The ranch literally becomes a winter wonderland. We can bring out the sleds."

"And how long does this fun last?"

"From the Friday after Thanksgiving until December twenty-third. Then we close up shop and the ranch is on vacation for nine days until January second."

Zach cocked his head. "Ranches don't close, Emma."

"I know but the administration building does and the phones are sent to voice mail and we only do the chores necessary to keep the ranch running. No lessons, no therapy appointments, no school."

Zach's phone rang, and he glanced at the screen and grimaced. *Ian's family.*

"Do you need to get that?"

"I'll call them back later."

Emma nodded. "I have to get moving anyhow. I still need to call the generator and lighting company to confirm reservations I made months ago." She looked at him. "Can I leave you with the lights?"

"What you mean is can you trust me with the lights?"

She put a hand on her hip. "Two weeks, Zach. That's all we have."

"Am I allowed to recruit a light team?"

"A strictly volunteer team."

"I can do that."

"Benjie and Mick?"

"I don't know anyone else," he returned.

A smile lifted the corners of her mouth. "This is going to be interesting."

"Wasn't that the point of all this?"

"Not quite, but I have faith you're going to understand the point of all this before we're done."

"It's good to have hope."

"Let me know when the lights are ready and I'll get the cherry picker scheduled."

"When do they need to be ready to go?"

"We have a lights-on practice the day before Thanksgiving and go live for the staff and children on Thanksgiving Day. Oh, and don't forget the greenery. Wreaths, garlands and swag will need to go up at the same time as the lights."

"Greenery?"

"I'll pick up the greenery at the nursery. They should be calling any day now."

"Is there a map or some sort of schematic on how the lights are to be put up?"

Emma pulled a sheet from the clipboard. "Here you go. Everything you need is right here."

He glanced through the computer-generated 3-D landscape map. "Impressive."

"Thank you." She grabbed her coffee. "I'll check back with you later."

"Much later, if you don't mind."

"The lights have to be ready to go by the day before Thanksgiving."

"I got that part. And that we have two weeks."

"That's right." She started down the stairs, one hand on the wall, the other balancing her clipboard and coffee cup.

"You forgot the muffins," Zach called.

"Those are for you."

He paused, touched by the gesture. "Thank you. Need help getting down those steps?"

"I've got it."

"Emma," he murmured.

She stopped and turned slightly.

"I can do the lights any way I want to just as long as it doesn't cost the ranch anything, right?"

"Zach, what are you up to?"

"Was that a yes?"

Emma shook her head and continued down the stairs. "It was a yes. A very nervous yes."

Now all he had to do was locate millions of LED outdoor lights and get them delivered ASAP. Zach grinned. Man, he loved a challenge.

Emma checked on the girls and wandered to the living room, where the weather report flashed across the muted television screen. Frost warning tonight. The possibility of snow on Thanksgiving.

That should have made her deliriously happy. Instead, melancholy filled Emma, and she didn't know why. She should have gone to bed an hour ago but an odd restlessness stirred inside tonight.

Stepping into the kitchen, Emma almost pulled out her cookbook, until Zach's words from earlier today floated back to her.

Therapeutic baking. Okay, yes, she had made an inordinate amount of chocolate chip and snickerdoodle cookies since the party on Monday. The staff was thrilled. But perhaps she did need to deal with what was bothering her. Except that she suspected Zach was at the root of everything keeping her awake.

She hadn't slept much at all since the Christmas party. Her mind continued to do a slow-motion play-by-play of the evening every time her head hit the pillow. First, there was dancing with Zach, and then that awkward moment when she nearly fell from the chair. Emma cringed just thinking about the incident.

Why couldn't things be simple like they used to be?

Her gaze went to the coffee table and the framed picture of herself with both Steve and Zach, taken years ago. So much happiness on that day.

A deep ache circled her heart and squeezed.

Though a solitary tear found its way down her face, a smile curled her lips, paying homage to this particular memory.

Every single day she missed Steve. He was her husband, but long before that, he was her friend. Being around Zach only reminded her that she had lost both Norman brothers. The fact was, not a day went by that she didn't miss Zach, too.

Now that he was back, she found herself confused by the feelings he stirred in her and the spark of awareness that was always present when he was near.

When the doorbell rang, her gaze went to the mantel clock. 10:00 p.m. She checked the peephole and blinked with surprise. Zach was on her porch.

Emma unlocked the door and pulled it open, reaching for the screen. "Zach?"

"Travis has been trying to reach you."

Anxiety tensed her fingers, and she fumbled with the lock on the screen door. "Come in. Come in. It's cold out there."

He wore a long-sleeve black sweater and jeans, and his hair was tousled, as though he'd dressed in a hurry.

Emma grabbed her phone from her tote bag hanging on the back of the dining room table. *Dead*. "I'm so sorry. Such a crazy day. The girls were crying and hungry and I tossed my purse and forgot about it..."

"Take it easy, Emma. It's okay."

"But Travis. Is Travis all right?"

"He's fine. He asked me to check on you."

"Why?"

"He's still working. Lucy tried to call you."

"Wait a minute." She shook her head and looked up at him. "Lucy is the one trying to reach me?"

"Not anymore. AJ went over to watch the triplets and Jack took Lucy to the emergency room."

Emma looked around the room, trying to figure out what to do next. "Can you stay with the twins and I'll go—"

"Hold on, let me finish." Zach put a hand on her arm. "Lucy is home now. Everything is fine. She's been put on modified bed rest as a precaution." He pulled his phone from his back pocket. "Travis wants you to call. Here, use my cell."

The tearful cry of one of the twins had Emma moving toward the hall.

Zach stepped in her path. "Call Travis. I'll look in on them."

"Are you sure?"

"Emma, I got this."

She took the phone and punched in Travis's number.

"Emma. Everything okay at the house of twins?"

"Dead cell. So sorry. Lucy?"

"Lucy's fine. The baby wants to make an appearance early, and the doctor is trying to slow things down. He's ordered what they call modified bed rest."

"You're sure that's all?"

"Yes. AJ talked to Jack and Lucy. Everything is under control, but I've forbidden her from coming to the ranch except for Thanksgiving dinner. She can work from the comfort of her couch at home."

"She listened to you?"

"I threatened to deactivate her security badge if she tried to come to work."

Emma laughed. "I'm so sorry I missed that conversation."

"Could I talk to Zach real quick?" Travis asked.

"Just a minute."

Emma moved quietly down the hall toward the girls' room and peeked inside, her eyes slowly adjusting to the darkness illuminated only by the soft glow of a night-light. Her heart tripped at the sight of the big navy SEAL hovering over the guardrail of her daughter's toddler bed. Zach had leaned down to rub Elizabeth's back in little circles and she murmured softly in sleep.

Was he humming? *He was.* Zach Norman was humming her baby to sleep.

Her hand went to her throat and she bit her lip at the unexpected tenderness of the scene before her.

"Zach?" she finally whispered. Emma nodded toward the cell in her hand, and he followed her to the living room.

"Travis." Emma spoke into the phone. "He's right here."

"Can you put the phone on speaker?" Travis asked.

Emma looked to Zach as she complied. "He wants the phone on speaker."

"I hate to ask," Travis said, "and I'm sorry

to put you on the spot, but I don't have much choice. With Rue Butterfield gone and Lucy on bed rest, we're down two staff members. Do you and Emma mind taking over Lucy's team?"

"What was Lucy in charge of again?" Zach asked. "Tell me it wasn't the live nativity, because Dutch said..."

Emma and Travis both started to chuckle.

"I didn't even finish telling you and you're already laughing. What's so funny?" Zach asked.

"Dutch got you with that mustache story," Travis said.

Zach blinked. "Are you saying that old codger pulled one over on me?"

"Dutch does it every year," Emma said.

"That cowboy better sleep with his eyes open." Zach shook his head. "But yeah, I'm happy to pick up the slack. Whatever you need. You can fill me in tomorrow." He looked to Emma. "I guess I should have asked Emma first. She's the one who has to work with me."

"It will be fine," she said. Because it had to be—the entire program depended on him.

"Great. Thank you," Travis said. "And Zach, you've probably saved the Holiday Roundup."

Zach's gaze met Emma's, and he rolled his eyes at the irony.

"Okay, I'll let you go. By the way, Emma, Lucy said the greenery is ready to be picked up tomorrow."

"I'll take care of it."

"Her team assignments for the tree sales are in her office." He chuckled. "Hope you can find them in that mess."

"Iris can dig them out for me."

"Great. Night, folks."

Zach turned to her. "Greenery tomorrow?"

She handed him his phone and nodded. "Yes. Baxter Farms. It's a nursery and fresh produce market between here and Pawhuska. You're welcome to come along."

"What time?"

"Right after lunch? I'll be bringing the girls because there's a petting zoo for children."

"You have animals on the ranch."

"Not sheep or donkeys."

He nodded. "I've got a lesson with Mick at four. Will we be back in time?"

"Oh, yes. This will take maybe two hours, tops."

"Then I'm in. Do you mind if we take my truck? There's more room for my knee."

"Not a problem, except that means I get to navigate."

Zach's eyes widened.

"I saw that."

"Emma, it's a documented fact that you're genetically direction challenged."

"This is only a few miles down the road."

"Yeah, that's what you said when we were going to the State Fair."

Her mouth dropped open for a moment and she stared at him. “That was years ago and it was in Tulsa. A town I was not familiar with.” She huffed. “I can’t believe you pulled that out of your saddlebag like it was yesterday.”

“Some memories refuse to die.”

“Well, relax. My cell phone provides excellent directions. No worries.”

“If you say so.” He moved toward the door, hands in pockets, then turned and glanced around. “Nice little house.”

“Thanks. I bought it after the girls were born.”

He nodded. “It’s you.”

“Is that a good thing?”

“Yeah, it’s comfortable, practical and feels like home.”

“Thank you.”

“I better get going.”

“Sure. You’ve got to be tired after saving Christmas at Big Heart Ranch.” Emma couldn’t help the small laugh that escaped.

Zach turned back, eyes narrowed. “I knew you wouldn’t let that slip past.”

“Well it’s not exactly, WWSD.”

“Excuse me?”

“What would Scrooge do?” She smiled. “I think you might be coming over to the green-and-red side.”

“You’re really on a roll, aren’t you?” he returned.

“Oh, come on. You have to admit, things are

sort of fun around here. You're going to miss all this when you leave."

He scoffed. "We'll see how I feel come January."

"What will you do in January?" she asked softly as stark reality reared its ugly head. "You said you have a job. What kind of job?"

"Security contracting. Overseas." Zach stared past her toward the twins' room.

Overseas? They'd never see him. "Is that what you want?" she asked.

He shrugged. "Emma, I don't know what I want anymore."

A chilly breeze whooshed past Emma when he pushed open the screen door and walked out into the night.

She closed the door behind him and leaned against the wood thinking about his response.

"Neither do I," she murmured. "Neither do I."

Chapter Five

Emma paced back and forth across the parking lot in front of the black pickup truck.

The girls were bundled into their stroller, sitting beneath a redbud tree whose branches were dressed in the remaining golden leaves of autumn. The toddlers' happy gibberish filled the air as they played with the identical plastic animals that Emma had pulled from the toy box to ensure a quiet trip. Next to the stroller, the car seats were stacked, and next to that, a large diaper bag was propped.

She'd barely had time to process Zach's sudden appearance in their life. Now she was going to spend the day with him?

What seemed like a good idea last night seemed a ridiculously impulsive invitation in the light of day. If she'd stopped to think this through, she would have realized that close proximity with Zach was not conducive to her peace of mind.

She could have gotten the greenery herself. In and out and no one gets hurt.

Emma stared at the cab of the truck, which was shrinking with each glance. She was stuck with Plan B and it terrified her.

"How'd you know which truck was mine?"

Her head popped up at the question. Zach strode across the parking lot, the limp less pronounced this afternoon. His hands were in the pockets of his jeans. He wore a dark blue sweatshirt with the word *Navy* emblazoned across his chest.

She glanced away, trying to remember that she was a mother with two children. A highly respected churchgoing member of the community. A business owner.

As such, she should not be noticing the breadth of a man's shoulders in a form-fitting sweatshirt, nor the dark stubble on his face that gave him an irresistible rogue look. Emma shivered.

"Hello? Anyone home?" Zach asked with a knuckle rap on the hood of his truck.

"Huh? Oh, sorry." She raised her head, grateful he couldn't read her mind. "I looked around for the baddest and most outrageously macho pickup," she said with an eye on the oversize truck. "This was the one."

"California plates gave me away."

Emma shrugged. "That, too."

"Have you been waiting long?" he asked.

"Just got here." She narrowed her gaze. "You seem unusually chipper."

"I get to spend time with my nieces."

"They've been here for the last twenty-eight months, you know."

Zach met her gaze. "I know, Em. But I couldn't get away."

"Couldn't or wouldn't? I mean, really? Three years and you couldn't get away?"

Zach bowed his head and stared at the ground for a moment. "I thought we had a holiday truce."

Emma closed her mouth, tamping down the unexpected rush of bitterness. Where had that come from anyhow? "Yes, right. Sorry."

An awkward silence stretched between them for a moment.

"So, um, how's Lucy? Have you heard from her?" Zach asked.

"I called this morning. She's feeling guilty about leaving us with her team and having a hard time keeping her fingers out of the roundup."

"Isn't there something she can do from home?"

"Yes. I turned over some of my phone calls to her."

"Good idea." Zach glanced at the twins and they responded by leaning forward to peek beyond the protective canopy of the double stroller at him. Wide-eyed, both toddlers craned their little necks to stare up at Zach with interest.

"They like being in that contraption?" he asked.

"Actually, they prefer to walk, but when we're in crowds or need to cover long distances, this contraption is safer for all of us."

He raised a brow.

"Don't judge," Emma said. "Chasing after two children sounds easier than it is."

"I'll take your word for it." Zach crouched down to eye level with the stroller, keeping his left knee stretched nearly straight. "Introductions?"

"Girls, this is Uncle Zach," she said. "He's going with us."

They continued to stare and Emma in return stared at them, dumbfounded. Good grief. It wasn't as if they'd never seen a man before. He was exactly like Travis, except the large economy size.

"Are they okay?" Zach asked.

"Yes." Emma snapped her fingers several times, and the twins finally looked at her. "Girls, can you say Uncle Zach?"

"Unca Zach."

"Which one was that?" Zach murmured.

"Rachel. She's wearing red and Elizabeth is in purple."

"Color-coded kids. I like that."

"Good, because I did it as a courtesy. Consider that your handicap until you can tell them apart."

"You said they're identical, except for a birthmark."

"This is true. However, they have quite different dispositions."

He narrowed his eyes and assessed them. “The other one doesn’t talk?”

“Elizabeth. Not the other one.” Emma shook her head. “Unless she has a horse in the race, Elizabeth lets Rachel do the work for her.”

“Smart kid.”

“Smart and clever.”

He stepped to the sidewalk and heaved a car seat over his shoulder. “So we put these in the truck, right?”

“Yes.” She pulled open the passenger door of the double cab and placed one in the back seat. Zach moved to the other side to do the same. Their hands collided as they searched for the seat belts.

Zach froze and jumped back as if he’d been zapped with a cattle prod. “Sorry, static electricity,” he murmured.

Is that what that was?

Head down, he clicked the seat belt into place.

“Are you okay with putting Rachel in her seat on your side?” Emma asked.

“I think the question should be ‘Is Rachel okay with me putting her in the car seat?’”

Emma nodded her head toward the twins. “Go for it. They’re still awestruck.”

“Okay, sure. I can do this.” He unbuckled the stroller restraint and Rachel immediately held out her pudgy little arms.

“You have a fan,” Emma observed.

When Zach wrapped his hands around Rachel and lifted her up, the two-year-old snuggled against his chest as though she belonged there. Zach froze, his eyes meeting Emma's.

"Is she okay?" he asked.

"Oh, yes," Emma said, as her heart melted around the edges. "I think it's safe to say that she likes you."

"Really?"

Emma cocked her head. "How could you possibly not realize that you leave a trail of swooning females wherever you go?"

Zach's eyes popped wide at her words. "Me? Not hardly." He carried Rachel around the truck to the car seat. She didn't resist when he put her in the car seat and buckled her in.

"She smells good," he said. "Baby perfume?"

"You can smell that?" Emma picked up Elizabeth and cuddled her daughter close. The lingering scent of sweetness and purity and babyhood had all but disappeared. Her babies were growing up so fast.

"That was much easier than I expected," Zach said.

"They're setting you up," Emma said as she fastened the connection on Elizabeth's car seat. "Even now, they're secretly plotting a diabolical plan to get you to let your guard down before the big strike."

When he glanced at Rachel and Elizabeth, they graced him a tender smile of adoration.

"Naw," he murmured. "These two are little princesses."

Emma snorted. "Right now you're a novelty and the little princesses are enamored. Wait until they realize you won't bend to their will upon demand. They can go from smiling to screaming in zero point sixty seconds. And always in the most embarrassing situations."

"You're making that up."

"You'll see," she returned with a singsong voice.

"What about the stroller?" Zach asked.

Depressing buttons, Emma quickly broke down the stroller. "Ready to go."

"That was impressive." Zach picked it up and put it in the bed of the truck as she slid into the passenger seat and shoved the diaper bag in front of her feet.

"What's in the suitcase?" he asked when he got into the truck.

Emma laughed. "That's a diaper bag."

He fastened his seat belt and put the key in the ignition. "That's a lot of diapers."

"This is my survival kit." She patted the canvas duffel. "I have everything necessary for any worse-case scenario created by toddlers in the wild."

"So you're sort of a SEAL yourself," Zach said.

She considered his words. "That's one way to look at it, except that my training program is much tougher than yours."

"I don't think so."

She smiled serenely. "Oh, plebe, you have so much to learn."

From the back seat, a voice spoke. "Momma duive, pease."

"Which one was that?"

"Elizabeth, the quiet, bossy one."

"What did she say?"

"She wants me to drive."

"Really?" He glanced in the rearview mirror. "That's what she said?"

"I'm fluent in toddler speak."

"Okay, so why does she want you to drive?"

"Because we're still sitting here."

His eyes rounded and he turned around in his seat to look at Elizabeth. "Whoa. Back seat driver?"

"Exactly. But she did say 'please.'"

Zach shook his head and reached across Emma toward the glove box. When his hand grazed her denim-clad knee, their gazes collided.

"Um, sorry," Zach murmured.

Emma inched closer to the door. "Is there something I can get for you in there?"

"My sunglasses."

Careful to avoid contact, Emma dangled the dark aviators from her fingers.

"So you're the copilot," he said as he slipped the glasses on. "Which way?"

"Just head out of the ranch and turn right."

"You're sure?"

"Relax," Emma said as she leaned back against the soft leather seat. "I've got this."

"Yeah. That's the part that concerns me," he murmured.

Once they were outside the long ranch drive, on a two-lane road and several miles from Big Heart, Zach glanced in the rearview mirror then turned to her. "What happened? They're both asleep."

She nodded. "It's some sort of quantum physics law. Put a child in a car and drive and they fall asleep. Sometimes I just drive around the ranch to settle them down."

"News to me," he said.

Emma smiled. "Me, too."

As they came to a four-way stop, Zach looked up and down the road. "Which way?"

"Keep going straight."

"You're sure? Because downtown Timber is to the right."

"I'm sure."

Minutes later, a large billboard advertising Baxter Farm came into view. Emma leaned forward and pointed out the window. "Hey, look. There's a sign. Two miles farther on your right."

"I thought you said you go every year. Why do you sound so surprised that the sign is there?"

She cleared her throat. "I may still have a few internal compass issues."

A low, deep laugh erupted from Zach. From his profile, she could see his eyes crinkle with the action. Emma's heart filled with an unknown longing at the sound. She hadn't heard Zach belly laugh in much too long.

Minutes later, as he parked the truck and she explained that besides the greenery she would need twenty poinsettias, Zach was no longer laughing.

"That many?"

"Yes. They'll fit in the bed of your truck nicely."

A grimace was his only response.

"Is there a problem?" she asked.

"What if those pots overturn?"

"They won't."

This time he frowned.

"If they do, I'll help you clean it up."

Zach's gaze followed the dozens of young children running over the grounds. "Why are there so many kids here?"

"It's Friday and there's a school bus parked across the street. It must be a field trip."

"Once again, my timing is off," he muttered. "Tell you what. I'll get the poinsettias and you and the girls go start the whole petting thing."

"Okay, but be sure to get the ones that look

lush with dark green leaves down to the soil line." With a hand on the stroller, Emma took a step and then hesitated. "Are you sure—"

"I'm trained to be combat ready. I can handle this." He nodded toward the animals. "Go pet a lamb or we'll never get out of here in time for my riding lesson with Mick."

Emma turned the stroller toward the fenced petting zoo area behind the fruit and vegetable market, dodging children as she traversed the dirt trail.

"Unca Zach?" Rachel asked. She turned in the stroller, her hands reaching for him as he headed in the other direction.

"Uncle Zach will be right back."

"Unca Zach!" Rachel began to scream.

"Rachel, he'll be right back." Emma knelt down next to her. "Look, the lambs are over there. Baa-baa, lambs. You love lambs."

"Unca Zach!"

Elizabeth's lower lip quivered and a fat tear rolled down her plump and rosy cheek. Before Emma could do anything, she began to wail, simply because Rachel was crying. In mere seconds, both children were inconsolable. Around Emma, people had stopped to stare.

Emma turned the stroller around and raced toward Zach.

"Zach! Zach, wait up."

He turned, stunned surprise registering on his face. "What's going on? Why are they crying?"

"Rachel is upset that you're leaving."

"I'm not leaving."

Rachel's cries only got louder, her face red with the effort, as her hands stretched toward Zach.

Crouching down, Zach unbuckled Rachel and pulled her into his arms. He stroked her back until she stopped crying.

Emma picked up Elizabeth. After a moment, the only thing left was soft hiccups.

"Sippy," Rachel said with a sniff. Emma handed Zach a red sippy cup and offered Elizabeth a purple one. Rachel wrapped her little fingers around the cup and drank in noisy gulps.

"Enough?" Zach asked when the toddler took a breath.

Rachel nodded.

"Should we all go for poinsettias?" Zach asked.

"Sure. Since my children can't live without you," she murmured.

"Who knew I was a toddler magnet?" Zach said with an embarrassed smile.

"Potty, Mommy," Rachel said.

"This is your department," Zach said. He slipped Rachel back into the stroller.

Emma did a full circle, glancing around until she spotted a restroom. She nodded to the right. "Let's go, girls."

"Don't need potty," Elizabeth said, her lower lip jutting out.

Emma rubbed the bridge of her nose and looked up at Zach. "Do you mind watching her while I take Rachel?"

"No problem."

Emma put Elizabeth on the bench behind them, stood Rachel on her feet and took her hand.

"Go ahead," he said as he eased down next to Elizabeth, his left leg stretched out. "We'll be fine."

Elizabeth looked at him from the corner of her eye and scooted to the end of the bench.

"I guess we know how she feels," he murmured.

"Watch her closely. She's wily, that one. I'll be right back." Emma shoved the giant diaper bag on her shoulder and took off.

Eager to return to Uncle Zach, Rachel was quick in the restroom. When Emma came back outside she heard Zach call out, "Wait." But he wasn't talking to her.

Elizabeth had jumped down from the bench and had quickly distanced herself from the former navy SEAL. The toddler became a blur of purple as her little legs moved furiously.

"Whoa, whoa, whoa," Zach called out. "Where do you think you're going?"

A mother with a stroller cut in front of him, and he nearly lost Elizabeth. Though he was limping, he picked up speed and caught the child around the waist.

Immediately, she began to howl. "I want my mommy." The cries escalated until her words became unintelligible watery sobs. Alarmed observers turned to stare at the toddler and the giant of a man who held her.

"Uh-oh! Zach needs help," Emma murmured. She scooped up Rachel, grabbed the stroller and diaper bag. Even race walking, she struggled to catch up with his long strides.

Finally, Zach stopped at a cotton candy kiosk. He picked a bag from the display and handed it to Elizabeth. Her small hand wrapped around the cone and the crying stopped midwail.

"Hey, pal, are you or your wife gonna pay for that?" the vendor asked, looking first at Zach and then to Emma, who'd finally reached him.

"My *what*?" Zach asked.

"I've got it," Emma said from behind him as the diaper bag slid to the ground with a thud.

Zach turned, opened his mouth and closed it. "You saw?" he finally said.

Emma nodded as her face warmed. "Yes. Well done. I'm thinking your SEAL training prepared you for this."

"Nothing could prepare me for this," Zach muttered as he removed the plastic wrapper from the treat. He looked at Elizabeth and pointed to the pink froth. "Cotton candy."

"Cottom canny," the toddler repeated. She stared with wonder at the soft pink puffs of spun sugar, then poked her finger into the cloud and released a watery giggle.

When Zach pinched off a small amount, Elizabeth opened her little bird mouth to accept the offering. Her eyes rounded and a smile lit up her face.

"More, please," she said.

He complied.

"More."

Emma leaned around him, took a piece of cotton candy and popped the treat into Rachel's mouth, as well.

He shifted Elizabeth to his other hip. "This is one tough assignment."

"Definitely not for wimps."

Zach shook his head. "How do you do it, Em?" he asked as they walked back to the bench.

"Do what?"

"All that you do? You're a single mom, and you have multiple jobs…"

"Each of us does what we have to do. Besides, Lucy and Travis have been there for me."

"My dad and stepmom?"

"It's been a rough couple of years for your folks. Don't be so hard on them. First, they lost Steve, then your stepmother's cancer diagnosis. They needed to get away from the ranch and escape."

"I'm your children's uncle. I should have been here."

"Then why did you stay away?" she dared to ask.

His head jerked slightly, and he turned to look at her before his attention refocused on the child in his arms. "I can't answer that yet. The last twelve months have been difficult. I'm still working through things."

"Maybe talking about it would help."

"Yeah, maybe. Just not today."

"Before you disappear from our lives again, then?"

"I won't disappear this time."

"Promise?"

His thoughtful gaze moved from Elizabeth to Rachel, and then to her. He offered a solemn nod. "I do."

Emma was silent, turning his words over in her mind. What would it be like to have Zach around all the time? Despite his words, she didn't believe it would ever happen. He didn't stay in one place long enough to even allow that thought to play out in her mind.

But what if? Emma shoved the question away. She wasn't ready to consider the possibility.

Zach let the glass door to the Big Heart Ranch administration building close behind him. He approached the reception desk, where the human resources woman sat smiling.

"Mr. Norman, good morning. Did you have a good weekend?"

"I did, thanks."

"Your staff T-shirts have arrived." She reached under the counter and handed him a neat stack of two red shirts.

"Red?"

"Yes. We issue red shirts once a year for the holiday season."

He held up the T-shirts with dismay before handing them back. They might fit his left bicep. "I'm going to let you keep these."

"I could order a larger size."

"Red isn't my color. But thank you." He glanced around. "Can you tell me where Emma's office is?"

"Straight down the hall, on the right, before you get to the conference room."

"Thanks."

"Mr. Norman, would you mind bringing Emma her lunch?" She nodded toward a large paper bag with the Timber Diner logo on the outside that sat on the counter.

"No problem." He picked up the neat sack, only to discover it was hefty. There had to be enough food in here to feed half of a SEAL team.

Zach peeked in the open doorways as he walked down the hall. One office, the size of a closet, had a sign that read Iris Banner, Administrative Assistant. Another belonged to Lucy Maxwell Harris. He walked past, then backed up and looked in again, not sure what to make of the chaos. It seemed that a tornado had swept through the room, leaving papers and books everywhere. Puzzled, he kept walking.

The next office on the right was Emma's. She looked up at his tap on the door and reached for a tissue. Today Emma was all dressed up in a pale gray suit with a silky blouse. Her long hair was anchored to the back of her head in a twist.

"Zach, what a surprise." Emma wiped her eyes, and then grinned widely, not quite meeting his gaze.

"Emma?" He placed the sack on the desk.

When she finally looked at him, he inhaled sharply. The pain in her red-rimmed eyes kicked him straight in the gut. His heart picked up speed as he shot straight into protective mode. "Hey, what's wrong?"

"I'm good," she murmured.

"No, you're not." He sat down in the chair on the other side of her desk. "What happened?"

"I…" She swallowed and balled up the tissue. "I just returned from court. The judge ruled in favor of the custodial parents. The child is being returned to an unthinkable home environment despite our pleas." She put a hand to her mouth. "It's an awful situation. Awful."

Without thinking, Zach stood to move around the desk, then knelt down next to her.

"Your knee."

"I'm only down on one knee." He paused, dumbstruck at the words that had slipped from his mouth.

She sniffed, thankfully oblivious to his awkward declaration.

"Emma, I'm so sorry." Zach handed her a tissue. When he gently pressed her head to his shoulder, he found himself surrounded by the soft flowery scent that was Emma. Not unlike dancing at the party, holding Emma was both oddly right and oddly terrifying.

"I should have been able to do more," she murmured.

There were no words. He, too, had been troubled by that same line of reasoning for months.

"Sometimes we can't do more," he said. "All we can do is turn it over to the Lord."

For a few moments she leaned against him, eyes closed, dark lashes splayed on her sun-kissed face.

Zach glanced around the office at the framed photographs of Big Heart Ranch children that covered the walls. Like they were her own children. And in a way, he supposed they were.

This was Emma's passion.

It wasn't baking or RanchPro. Big Heart Ranch was her calling. Her ministry. The realization made him all the more restless and uncertain of his future. What was the Lord calling him to do with the rest of his life?

When Emma put inches between them and looked at him, her dark eyes were watery and vulnerable. Zach froze, captivated and speechless. This was why he avoided falling into the depth of Emma's gaze. Every single time, he found himself drowning in emotions he was unprepared to deal with.

"I'm sorry," she whispered. "I never cry."

"You shouldn't feel like you have to be the ambassador for happy all the time. You do so much for so many. It's okay to be real with me. We go too far back for that." Zach reached out to slip a loose tendril of silky brown hair behind her ear and immediately regretted the gesture.

He knew better.

Silence stretched between them and Zach used the opportunity to grab the desk edge. He bit back a grimace when the patchwork of scars, muscles and ligaments complained as he heaved himself to a standing position. Emma was worth the pain.

It took only a moment for her to shift back to the perpetually positive and smiling Emma persona she put on for the world.

Her hands settled in her lap and she looked at him. "You stopped by to see me?" she asked.

"Yeah, I found this in my truck this morning." He pulled out a neon purple toy animal from his back pocket and squeezed the soft plastic until it squeaked. "I figured this could be a matter of national security."

A slow smile touched her lips. "Thank you."

"Oh, and I brought your lunch." He pointed to the bag on the desk.

"You brought my lunch?" Her eyes rounded.

"From the front desk, that's all. What do you have in there? That sack is huge. Smells good, too."

"BLT and fries from the diner. Want some?"

He shook his head. "I'm not going to eat your lunch."

"There's two and a half lunches in there. We have a standing order with the diner for Fridays and lately, Lucy orders extra." She smiled. "You know, for the baby."

"Sure. Right. Eating for two."

Emma unfolded the edges of the bag. "And they always add cookies, whether I ask for them or not."

He leaned forward to peek inside the bag. "What kind of cookies?"

"Does it matter?"

"Probably not," he said.

Emma pulled out a foam box of cookies and slid it across the desk. "Here."

Zach sat down again and opened the container, eyes rounding at the sight. "Chocolate chip. My favorite."

"I remember. And these were made today. Go ahead and take Lucy's lunch and the cookies with you."

"What about you?"

"I'm happy with my sandwich." She grabbed her water bottle from the desk. "Do you want anything to drink?"

"Naw, I'm good." Zach nodded in the direction of the hallway. "What are they doing to Lucy's office?"

"What do you mean?" She took a swig of water.

"It looks like it's under construction."

Emma inhaled and began to cough on a laugh.

"Are you okay?" Zach started to move around the desk.

Holding up a hand, she stood and thumped her chest. "Yes. Give me a second." The words were more like a croak. A moment later, she sat down and wiped her eyes. "Oh, my. I need a warning next time."

"What? I only asked if her office—"

"That's another day for Lucy. The normal state of things. Although it has gotten better since we hired Iris."

"Seriously? Your sister always seems so efficient."

"She is efficient, with a very unusual organizational system."

"Right." He glanced at the clock on her wall.

"Was there something else?"

"Yeah. I want you to know I'm thinking…" He

paused and cleared his throat. "I'm thinking of taking a look at Steve's business."

"RangePro."

"Yeah."

Emma's eyes widened and when she lifted her chin to look at him, he knew immediately what she was thinking. He shook his head. "No, Emma."

"You don't even know what I'm going to say."

"Oh, yeah, I do." He glanced at the clock again and stood. "This is not a commitment. I've come to realize that you have way too much on your plate. So I'm willing to open a discussion. Period."

"Okay," she said ever so slowly.

Zach swallowed, already feeling the room closing in on him. "I've got to be somewhere. We can talk about it later."

"When later?"

"One step at a time, Emma."

She released a breath of frustration. "How are the lights coming along?"

"Good. Good." And they were. The shipment of lights was on schedule to be delivered to the hardware store in Timber tomorrow.

"Good enough to rent the cherry picker?"

"Ah, I'll evaluate the situation and let you know."

"Today? You'll let me know today?"

"I can promise to have a definitive answer tomorrow."

"Okay, then. Tomorrow. Thank you."

Zach stepped toward the door.

"Zach?" she called.

He turned back.

She stood and handed him the cookies and the bag with the extra sandwich. "And um, I appreciate…you know…the kind words." She blinked, pink tinging her cheeks.

"Emma, you deserve so much more than kind words."

Zach hurried his steps, moving as fast as his knee allowed, running from complications before they had a chance to tackle him to the ground.

Chapter Six

"Of all the rude things." Emma continued to mutter under her breath as she approached her SUV in the shared parking lot between the Timber hardware store and the Busy Needle Fabric Shop.

She shifted her shopping bags to her other arm and moved to examine the clearly visible bright white lines painted on the pavement. It was obvious that the black truck that had pulled in backward violated proper parking etiquette.

"You're taking up two spaces, mister." Not only that, she couldn't open her car door.

Emma stopped when she got closer and recognized the license plate. "Zach? Seriously?"

The back door of the hardware store swung open and none other than Zach Norman walked out with a huge cardboard shipping box balanced on a shoulder. And the man was whistling a holiday tune! She'd never seen his face so animated.

Behind him, Mick Brewer followed, carrying a second box, along with a young clerk who carried yet a third box.

Emma stepped into view as Zach dug in his pocket for his keys.

"Need any help?" she asked.

Startled, Zach froze. His head slowly came up to meet her gaze. "Emma?"

"That's a lot of boxes, gentlemen."

When Mick laughed, Zach shot him a death stare.

"What do you have there?" Emma persisted. She stretched on her toes to peek over Zach's shoulder when he placed his box in the truck's bed and helped Mick do the same with his.

The man was much too large. She couldn't even see around his shoulder.

"They're—" Mick began.

"A holiday surprise," Zach finished for him.

"A holiday surprise? Is that so?" Emma asked.

"Yes, ma'am." Mick nodded furiously. "What he said."

"What about the rest of the boxes?" the store clerk asked as he, too, eased the box in his arms into the flatbed.

"There's more?" Emma raised a brow.

"I'll get them," Mick said. His eyes were wide as he backed his way to the store, his gaze moving back and forth between Zach and Emma as though he was watching a tennis match.

Zach stood like a flannel-and-denim giant with his hands on his hips blocking her view of the boxes. "I see you've been shopping," he said. "What's the occasion?"

"Are you kidding me?" Emma gently let all six of her shopping bags slip to the ground.

"Not that I'm aware of."

"Zach, I've been Christmas shopping."

"Once again I feel compelled to let you know that Thanksgiving isn't here yet."

"It's next week. Everyone knows that Christmas shopping should be completed by Black Friday. Cyber Monday at the latest, so you can enjoy Giving Tuesday."

Zach blinked. "There are rules?"

"Yes. Of course." She waved a hand in the air. "Look around you. The town is dressed from head to toe in garland, lights and holiday cheer. The spirit of giving is in the air, Zach."

"I'm concerned about what's in the water."

Emma released a sound of frustration and reached for her shopping bags.

"Need some help?"

"I've got the bags." She opened the hatch on her SUV. "But I can't get in my car. Your truck is blocking my driver's-side door."

With a slow nod, he walked around both parking spaces assessing the situation. "You parked too close to the line."

"I most certainly did not." She crossed her

arms over her chest. "How did Mick get out of the truck anyhow?"

"He's smaller than you are."

Emma gasped, and in a split second, she was seeing a bright red and that had nothing to do with Christmas. She glanced down at her jeans and cheerful holiday sweater. Okay, maybe she did still have a few pounds of "I had a baby" pudge to lose.

"I..." She opened her mouth and then closed it, meeting Zach's gaze.

He cleared his throat. "That may have come out wrong."

"Could you please move your vehicle?" she asked.

"Are you mad?" He raised a hand in gesture. "I wasn't insinuating that you're, um, not small."

"You should probably stop while you're ahead and just move the truck."

Zach stepped aside and Emma got a good look at the print on the boxes in the flatbed.

She whirled around. "I can't believe what I am seeing. Zachary Richard Norman, you bought LED lights. I told you we can't afford them."

"Anyone ever tell you that you sound just like someone's mother?"

"Don't change the subject."

"I'm not." He wedged himself between her and the boxes. "The lights were donated." His words were a low rumble.

"A million lights donated?" Emma paced back and forth in front of him, doing the math. "Those must have cost a small fortune. I can't even imagine who you had to fast-talk to get that sort of donation."

Suddenly, Emma stopped talking and looked up at him. The answer was right in front of her.

"You?"

He nodded.

"You can't do that. You're unemployed." She shook her head.

"First, I am hardly destitute or without means, and if you recall, Big Heart Ranch is my current employer."

"Certainly not the paycheck you normally pull."

"It's a donation. Let it go. I consulted with the ranch attorney and everything is legal."

"You spoke with Jack Harris and conveniently failed to check with me?"

"I did run this by you. I asked if I could do things my way as long as my way didn't cost the ranch anything."

"Implied consent. Oh, that was low."

Zach chuckled. "Only from your point of view. Maybe you should consider this part of that spirit of giving you were lecturing me about."

She sighed, her head drooping with defeat. He'd beat her at her own game. "This was very generous, albeit uncalled for, Zach. Thank you."

"There's a begrudging thank-you if ever I heard one."

"Comes with the territory. All the Maxwells have control issues."

"And you're admitting it?"

Emma scoffed. "I'm the only Maxwell that does. And that's just because I have a couple of degrees that say I understand my issues. Plus, I've got my own therapist."

"No kidding?"

"All part of the job description. I can't help others if I'm not willing to help myself."

"That's really great, Emma."

"Would you like her number?"

He narrowed his eyes. "Funny."

"I wasn't trying for humor."

"Well, FYI, I've been there and completed therapy. So no, thank you."

"You have?" Emma blinked at the admission.

When Mick stepped out of the store with two boxes on a hand truck, the conversation ended. "Everything okay out here?" He shot each of them a hesitant glance.

"Of course it is, Mick," Emma said.

Mick looked to Zach for confirmation. "Miss Emma is thrilled about the surprise lights."

The boy's face brightened. "Pretty cool, aren't they, Miss Emma? And Mr. Zach said I can help put them up."

"Yes, Mick, they are." She couldn't help but

notice the change in the boy. Once sullen, he was now a carefree kid. That was Zach's doing.

"You're working with a navy SEAL? Wow, I'm impressed, Mick," Emma continued.

"Former navy SEAL," Zach said quietly from behind her.

"You're much too modest," Emma returned, her voice equally soft. She turned to him. "Now may I rent the cherry picker? Lights-on is in one week."

"Sure. I'm ready." He offered a self-satisfied grin. "Since I have all new lights."

"Don't push it, pal." She paused. "Dutch offered to drive the crane if you'll ride in the basket. He's afraid of heights."

"Works for me."

She couldn't resist a smile. "Does this mean you're getting into the holiday spirit?"

He jerked back slightly. "No. Why would you think that?"

"You were smiling and humming a holiday song a few minutes ago."

"Subliminal programming. It's a week before Thanksgiving and the hardware store is blaring jingle, snowflake and merry nonstop. I can't be held responsible for that."

Emma laughed. "Oh, please, you're starting to become a Christmas cheer believer and you know it."

"Don't order me a Team Ho-Ho-Ho T-shirt just

yet, Emma. I don't want you to be disappointed." He tossed his keys into the air and caught them. "Now, why don't I move my truck for you?"

Emma's gaze moved to follow Mick, who had already deposited his box in the pickup bed and returned the hand truck to the store. Now he slipped into the space between the vehicles to claim his shotgun spot in the cab.

Okay, so he was smaller than her. When her glance returned to Zach, he raised his hands.

"I didn't say a thing."

"Right. Just move the truck," she muttered.

"See you back at the ranch, then, I guess," Zach said.

"I have to do a little Christmas shopping in Pawhuska. It will be a while."

"More shopping? Seriously?"

"I've already explained that."

He narrowed his gaze as though thinking. "Your status as a professional shopper might be to my advantage."

"How so?"

"I don't suppose you could do me a favor while you're out hunting and foraging in the wild for Christmas presents?"

She shot him a weak smile. "What sort of favor?"

"I need a gift for the parents of a friend of mine."

"Could you be a little more specific? What sort of gift?"

"I don't know. A holiday present." He grimaced. "I've only met them once before and it was on base."

"Could you ask your friend what his parents might like?"

"My friend died, that's why I'm stopping in to see them." His face was set in grim lines as he released the words.

Emma's hand shook as she raised her fingers to her lips, but she swallowed the grief clogging her throat. "Oh, Zach, I'm so sorry."

He nodded. "You know what? Forget it. No big deal."

"But it is a big deal and I want to help."

His eyes darkened. "Emma, I'm not one of your kids."

"But you *are* one of my friends, despite your protests to the contrary. Why don't you and I do a little shopping next week? Maybe after you get the lights up?"

Zach was silent for a moment as if considering her words.

"Where do your friend's parents live?" Emma persisted.

"Between Timber and Pawhuska."

"Wonderful. We can plan to stop in and see them on the way home."

He frowned, and his expression said he felt anything but wonderful about her suggestion.

"Zach, this can't be an easy visit. Let me go

with you for moral support." She paused, then continued, choosing her words with care. "I'm one of the few people who understands what you're going through."

His jaw clamped down and he stared straight ahead for a moment.

Emma put a hand on his arm. "Please, I'd like to be there for you."

Zach released a shaky breath. "I'll call you when the lights are up."

"Okay, then." Emma blinked. She could do this. She was a trained counselor. There wasn't a day that went by that she didn't help children work through grief issues.

Why did it seem different because…well, because it was Zach? The brother of her husband. The husband whose death she still grieved.

Self-talk. That's what she needed. Of course, she could put aside her own issues to be there for him.

Oh, Lord, she silently prayed. *I'm going to need some help.*

"Looks like our time is up," Zach said.

"Can I try to rope the dummy steer today, Mr. Zach? Please?" Mick's eager tone matched the grin on his face as he sat confidently on Grace, the sorrel mare he was once terrified of. "I've been practicing."

"Sure. Go ahead."

Mick eyed the bright green plastic steer in the middle of the pen with determination.

"On the ground, buddy. That's how we all start. Once you master that, we'll work on roping in the saddle."

Mick slid from Grace. He grabbed his rope from the saddle, strode to the center of the corral and concentrated on prepping the rope.

"That's it," Zach said. "Take your time. Make your loop. Remember what we talked about."

Mick confidently adjusted the rope in his gloved hand and began to practice swinging.

"Swing out a little farther, like you're tossing a baseball."

The boy nodded. He paused and stared down the steer before he released the loop. The lasso sailed through the air, catching the steer around the neck and left horn.

For a moment Mick stared at the steer with disbelief. Then his fist shot into the air. "I did it! I did it!"

"You sure did!" Zach gave a loud whoop and holler. "And the crowd goes wild. Can you hear them cheering for you?"

The ten-year-old pivoted around on his boots, kicking dust and sand into the air. "I can. I can hear it." A grin split his face.

"Take a look at that steer. See how the rope is around the neck and left horn? That's a half-head catch, and it got you on the leaderboard, buddy!"

"Yes, sir."

"I never doubted it for a minute." Zach glanced at his watch. "Keep practicing and you'll be ready for the Big Heart Ranch Summer Rodeo."

"Yes, sir." He offered a goofy grin.

Zach nodded toward the fence where Benjie had appeared to watch. "How're things with you and your brother?" he asked quietly.

"Aw, okay. He's just annoying sometimes, 'cause he's real smart and I'm not." Mick pulled his rope from the steer and began to coil it up.

"You're real smart, Mick."

"Not like Benjie. He's book smart."

"Don't compare yourself to your brother. You're Mick, the soon-to-be rodeo champ. God made you to be different from your brother and that's a good thing."

"You have a brother?"

"Yeah. A little brother. He died."

Mick looked up from the rope in his hands. "Do you miss him?"

"Every single day. I wish I had been a better big brother to him."

"How do you be a better big brother?"

"You have to look out for them, and love and protect them." Zach took a deep breath as he remembered Steve's smiling face when he'd pulled another prank. "Most of all, you have to remember that annoying you is a little brother's job."

"Yes, sir." Mick paused. "Are you coming back to the stable?"

Zach lifted his face to the cloudless blue sky. "Winter will be dancing into town real soon. Not many more days like this. I do believe I'm going to take a ride." He turned to Mick. "Tripp is in his office if you need any help with Grace."

"Oh, me and Grace are good buddies now."

"That's what I want to hear." Zach carefully mounted Zeus, guarding his knee. He stroked the chestnut gelding's mane. "Ready for a ride, boy?"

The animal snorted softly and offered a contented nicker.

"Hey, Zach, wait up."

He turned at Emma's voice to see her ride up next to him on Rodeo. Today the cowgirl wore a denim jacket and jeans with a pink plaid Western shirt. Her long hair was in a braid and a dark Stetson was on her head. Did the woman ever look anything but beautiful? Zach glanced away.

"How did you and Dutch do yesterday with the cherry picker?" she asked.

"No problems. The lights and the greenery are in place."

"I know. I checked."

He frowned. "Then why did you ask if you already knew?"

"I wanted to know if there were any problems I should be aware of."

"Not a one. We're ready for lights-on."

"Dutch said you finished in record time."

"Had help."

"Mick and Benjie and half the boys' ranch?" A slow smile of amusement warmed her face.

"Aw, now you're exaggerating again."

"How did you get all those boys to help you?"

He adjusted his ball cap and put a hand on the pommel. "Emma, I'm not going to tell you all my secrets."

"You bribed them."

"Hear that, Zeus? Now she's insulting me." Zeus stepped back at the words and offered a heavy grunt.

"Not at all," Emma said. "I'm curious. The word is that the boys were jockeying for a chance to work with you."

He raised a gloved hand in gesture. "I offered a lesson in commerce. Supply and demand."

When the chocolate-brown eyes rounded with realization, Zach did his best to bite back a laugh.

"You paid them!"

"It was on-the-job training. A life lesson. Hard work deserves a fair wage."

Emma slowly shook her head. "I should never have asked a question I really didn't want the answer to." She glanced around. "Are you going for a ride?"

"Thought I might."

"Mind if I join you?"

"Not at all."

"Where are you headed?"

Zach picked up the reins. "I'm letting Zeus decide."

"I hope he knows that." Emma followed, and they rode in companionable silence over the golden autumn pasture grass and then along a well-worn riding trail. The only sound was the dull clop of hooves on the dry red Oklahoma dirt.

"Bison paddock to your right," she called out after thirty minutes.

"Bison." Zach shook his head. "All females."

"How'd you know?"

"The beards gave it away."

Her laughter spilled into the silence. "Spot on, cowboy!"

With a tongue cluck to Rodeo, the horse and rider spurred ahead of Zach. "Oh, look. There's a tire swing. I forgot it was here." She pointed to the fence up ahead and the pond and the shade of a group of conifers. "Let's stop here."

She dismounted and stared across the fence to the neighboring ranch pastures, where cattle dotted the land.

"Such a shame. I remember when there was no fence this far north."

"Progress. It was destined to happen."

"Still, it's too bad. Remember how we used to roam all over the Pawhuska spread without even a cell phone?"

"I do."

Emma reached into her jacket pocket and pulled out a foiled wrapped packet. "Cookie?"

"You have cookies in your pocket?" He took the proffered treat.

"I like to be prepared."

"Do you have coffee, too?"

"I have a couple bottles of water." She reached into her saddlebag and tossed him a bottle. "Packed them when I did herd check this morning."

Zach unscrewed the lid and took a long pull. "You're working today?"

She nodded. "I gave AJ and Travis the day off. It's their one-month anniversary."

"One month? Is that a milestone?"

"When you're in love it is."

He rolled his eyes and declined comment. Sure, he could remember being goofy in love once. With Emma. That, too, was a long time ago.

"Where are the twins?" he asked.

"With a sitter. One of our college students from the girls' ranch helps me out. Gives her some extra income. A win-win."

"Emma, how is it a win-win when you never take a day off?"

"This is a family-run ranch and when we're short handed we all pitch in."

"That didn't answer my question."

She shrugged. "What can I say? It's a busy

time of year so most of the time I'm only off on Sundays."

"Yeah, but it seems you're here 24/7. When do you get a life?"

"Zach, this *is* my life."

She sat down on the ground and leaned against the rough bark of a small loblolly pine. "So, what about visiting your friend's parents? Want to try for tomorrow after church?"

"Doesn't seem fair to ask you on your only day off. What about Rachel and Elizabeth?"

"It's only a few hours."

"Let's bring them with us," Zach said.

Her eyes lit up. "Are you sure?"

"Joe and Mary will love seeing children. They're plain folks. Farmers. I'll call and let them know we'll be by."

Emma handed him the last cookie. "I have an idea for a gift."

"Oh?"

She met his gaze. "Aren't you going to sit down?"

"If I sit down with this knee, I won't be able to get up."

Emma easily stood. "Have you got a picture of you and your friend? Maybe on your phone?"

Zach pulled out his cell and slid a finger over the screen.

"I thought we could print it on the ranch copier. We have photo paper." She glanced at him. "I picked up a silver frame when I was in town."

"I like that idea. I like it a lot." Zach scrolled through the photos.

Emma peeked over his shoulder. "Is that him?"

"Yeah. Ian." Zach swallowed. He had to catch himself before his emotions shot out of control. "We'd been together since SEAL training, you know. Both of us knew catfish, ranches and Oklahoma college football. Hard to find another person in California who appreciated the fact that the world's largest McDonald's is in Vinita, Oklahoma. An impenetrable bond of Okie-ness."

She smiled. "Yes. I totally get that."

Zach lowered his head as an ache circled his heart. "He should be here now. Not me."

Emma sucked in a breath. "No. Don't say that. Don't even go there."

"You don't know…"

"I do know. I've been through more than my share of what-ifs. They'll destroy you, if you let them, Zach." She released a sigh. "I was supposed to go to town the day of the accident, but I was having morning sickness. Steve went instead." Emma's voice hitched as she took a breath. "It should have been me."

Zach's head jerked up, and he met her pained gaze. "No, Emma."

"It's not any different than what you're thinking."

"Yeah, but you don't know Ian. He was smart. Like Steve. So much to give the world."

"It's a tragedy that the world lost Ian and for that matter Steve. Your little brother was brilliant." A musing smile touched her lips as if she'd wrapped her mind around a memory.

For a moment Zach found himself jealous of the memories between Emma and Steve.

"But, I can tell you, the man didn't have a lick of common sense," Emma said. She chuckled. "It was a standing joke between us. He could explain things I didn't even understand in his computer techy lingo and then forget to take out the trash."

Zach smiled. "I never thought I'd hear you say that."

"What? I loved Steve, but he certainly wasn't perfect."

"I figured you thought he was."

She stared him down. "No, Zach, you're the one who put him on a pedestal."

He considered her words.

"Did I?"

"Yes," she said softly.

Had he put the distance between his brother and himself? The thought was sobering at best. At worst, a revelation that he'd wasted a lot of time owning emotions he shouldn't have.

"Do you ever visit your father's ranch?" Emma asked. "Relive all those memories from when we were kids?"

"That's a whole other topic, and I wouldn't

call it reliving memories. More like revisiting the scene of the crime."

She looked at him. "No good memories?"

"I'm still sorting through things."

"Why didn't you stay and take over your dad's ranch? Steve wasn't interested, but you were born a cowboy."

"I learned long ago that it was best for everyone if I stayed away." Zach glanced up at the sky when the sound of a hawk circling interrupted his musings. "Getting late," he said. "We better head back." He nudged Zeus forward and away from the discussion.

"Sure." Emma grabbed Rodeo's reins and mounted.

"Thanks for riding with me, Em," he murmured.

"I should be thanking you," she said. "I needed this break as much as you did."

Yeah, maybe he did need it. He'd only meant to exercise Zeus and catch fresh air. Instead, he'd taken a ride to his past and maybe started to clear out the cobwebs so he could think about the present. Maybe even the future.

Chapter Seven

"Emma, I'm not so sure this is a good idea," Zach said. His voice sounded hollow and dull to his own ears. He gripped the steering wheel with one hand while he stared at the modest farmhouse in front of them and willed his pulse to slow.

"Zach, you're parked in their driveway and they're peeking out of the front window at us. You can't turn around now."

"Sure I can." He nodded firmly. "Absolutely, I can."

Train in advance. Prepare in advance. He was failing on all fronts. His mental preparedness for surviving and enduring any life-threatening situation went down the tubes the minute they pulled into the Clarks' gravel drive.

"The twins will provide a buffer," Emma said. "Everyone likes babies."

Terrific, now he was hiding behind toddlers.

When Emma placed her small hand over his, he held his breath but didn't answer.

She gently pried his fingers free from the steering wheel. "We've got this, Zach."

His lip curled in what started as a smile and ended up as a snarl. It didn't escape him that he was a former navy SEAL being comforted by a petite cowgirl. He could chalk today up to a good initiative but bad judgment. His own doing.

It was time to face the sad reality that today was the day he'd been dreading.

Man up, pal, he told himself.

Zach glanced into the back seat. "The girls are asleep."

"And they'll stay that way if we're very careful. The church nursery followed by lunch always conks them out. Plus, Pastor Parr was a bit long-winded today." She nodded toward the house. "You bring in their play yard and they'll probably sleep through the entire visit."

Zach eased out of the truck and stretched his legs. He moved through Emma's instructions by rote and walked up to the front door with the twins' gear in one hand and a shopping bag with items for the Clarks in the other.

For a few moments, he stood on the threshold looking around the welcoming yard. This was Ian's house.

Ian, who would never come home again.

Zach had been hospitalized during Ian's memorial service. Never gave his buddy a proper goodbye.

A wave of emotion gripped him like a vise. It was Steve's funeral all over again.

Zach raised his head. Except, maybe this time he could ease someone else's pain. He wouldn't let the Clarks down like he'd let Emma and the twins down.

He rang the bell.

Ten minutes after being ushered into the house by Mary and Joe Clark, he realized Emma was right. *Again.* The Clarks were thrilled to have children, sleeping or awake, in their farmhouse. The mood in the home was nothing short of joyous as Ian's parents stood over the play yard admiring the sleeping toddlers.

"We don't have any grands to fuss over. This is a real treat," Mary Clark said. "And it sure doesn't hurt that they're simply adorable times two."

Joe Clark stood behind his wife with his hands on her shoulders, peering down at the twins. "Can't hardly remember when Ian was that small. We had him sort of late in life."

Mary laughed and patted her husband's hand. "What Joseph means is that Ian was a complete surprise. A blessing, but we were gobsmacked when we found out."

Zach smiled at the couple. After forty-seven years together, they sort of looked alike. Of sturdy build, they both had curly gray hair and weathered faces from good honest work. They were people of the land, Godly folks.

People who believed marriages lasted forever.

"Come and sit down in the kitchen," Mary said. "Now, how is it you two are related?"

"Emma married my half brother. We lost him three years ago."

"I'm so sorry." Mary clucked her tongue. "But I can see now why those babies look so much like Zach here." She smiled. "And you're so good with them for a single fella."

"The girls only have eyes for their Uncle Zach when he's around," Emma said.

"That might be a slight exaggeration," he mumbled.

"Emma Maxwell Norman. Now, why does the name Maxwell sound so familiar?" Mary asked as she put a tray of coffee and cake on the big farmhouse kitchen table and began to serve them.

"My family runs Big Heart Ranch in Timber."

"That's you? The children's ranch we've heard so much about?"

Emma nodded.

"What a beautiful ministry, Emma," Mary said. She carefully cut the cake and placed generous slices on mismatched china dessert plates, then nodded to her husband. "Pass this to our guests, dear."

"What kind of cake is this?" Emma asked.

"My special hummingbird cake." Mary smiled. "Guaranteed the best cake you've ever eaten."

"Hummingbird?"

"Sweet enough to attract hummingbirds, they say."

"Try it," Zach said. "Mary brought one to Ian when they visited California. I bought a couple pieces from him."

Mary burst out laughing. "That rapscallion. He sold my cake?"

"Yes, ma'am, and it was worth every penny."

"That's our Ian," Mary said. "Never missed an opportunity."

"Mary, doesn't the pastor send donations to Big Heart Ranch?" Joe Clark asked as he stirred sugar into his coffee cup.

"Pastor Cleveland?" Emma asked.

"Yes," Mary said with a nod. She slid a plate to her husband and sat down next to Emma.

"He helps us with the summer program every year. We certainly appreciate that."

When Emma paused and shot a speculative glance at Zach, he frowned at the expression on her face. What was she up to?

"Have you been to the ranch?" Emma asked the couple.

"Oh, no. I didn't think you allowed visitors," Mary said.

"A few times a year we're open to the public. The summer rodeo and our Holiday Roundup."

"That's coming up then," Joe said.

"Yes. The Holiday Roundup opens next Friday." Emma's eyes sparkled with contained excitement at the mention of her favorite subject. "What are you two doing for Thanksgiving?"

"Oh, it's just us and the cats," Mary said. "Most years Ian was out of the country. We got used to that."

"Will you join us at the ranch for Thanksgiving dinner?" Emma asked.

"On such short notice? That would be a terrible inconvenience for you."

"Not at all. My family and some of our staff all celebrate the holiday with dinner in the ranch chow hall. We don't take a head count. The day is purely potluck. Our equine manager, Tripp, brings the turkey and everyone else brings their personal specialties. It's a simple down-home meal."

Zach observed the exchange in awe. In a short period of time, Emma had warmed the Clarks' hearts and made friends.

Mary turned to her husband. "What do you say, Joseph?"

He narrowed his eyes in thought before he finally spoke. "Will there be pie?"

"Much too much pie, I'm afraid," Emma said with a slow shake of her head.

Joe Clark grinned. "That's the ticket. Save us a seat at the table."

Emma clapped her hands. "Wonderful. We turn the Holiday Roundup Christmas lights on after dinner. You'll get a preview before we open to the public."

"Well, I never. I feel like we're VIPs," Mary said.

"And you are."

Zach stared dumbfound. Was there anyone or any situation she couldn't finesse? The woman had a gift. She made everyone feel special, and it came from her heart. He could probably take a lesson from Emma.

For minutes, he sat silently enjoying the conversation and the reprieve. When the chatter lagged, he cleared his throat, pushed back his cake plate and coffee cup and looked to Ian's parents, knowing it was time to do what he came here for.

"Um, Mary. Joe. I brought you a few things," Zach said.

"I should wait in the truck," Emma said. Her eyes flitted to Zach, concern in the warm depths.

Zach put his hand on her arm as she began to stand.

"If Joe and Mary don't mind, I'd like you to stay, Emma." Zach swallowed. He wanted… No, he needed Emma to at very least understand the last twelve months of his life.

"If that's what you want, Zach," Mary said.

He nodded, opened the bag he brought with him and took out a sweatshirt and a worn silver cross on a heavy silver chain. "These were Ian's. He left them at my apartment when we did an Ironman event last winter."

Mary carefully took the sweatshirt and held the fabric to her face. She closed her eyes and inhaled, offering a bittersweet smile. "Smells like my Ian." With the back of her hand, she swiped at the moisture in her eyes. "Oh, Zach, thank you."

Joe Clark fingered the simple cross, his calloused fingers rubbing back and forth over the smooth surface.

"You need to know that Ian remained the pure-hearted man you raised him to be. He loved God and his country and both of you." Zach paused to swallow back emotion. "Every chance he got, he talked about the farm and his parents."

Mary turned to her husband and took his hand.

"I know you received the official report, and the navy presented you with the Navy Cross in his honor, but you need to hear it from me…

"That day…" Zach paused yet again. Though he'd practiced over and over again, and prayed about this moment, the words stuck in his throat. "That day, Ian never hesitated for a moment. He gave his life for his teammates.

"I tried to get to Ian, but an explosion… A cement block landed on my knee. I couldn't get out of the rubble in time to reach him." Chest tight, Zach closed his eyes for a moment and then glanced away. "I'm so sorry."

"Oh, Zach," Mary said. She stood, walked over to him and wrapped her arms around him. It took everything in him not to break down and blubber like a baby.

"That's why you're limping," Joe observed.

Zach nodded. "Yeah. I'm a civilian now."

"I'm sorry, son."

"Today isn't about me," Zach murmured. He handed Mary a flat white box. "I brought you something else. Emma helped me put this together."

Mary Clark's blunt fingers trembled as she opened the box and unfolded the tissue to reveal the silver frame with a picture of Zach and Ian in uniform, arms looped around each other. Joseph leaned close to peer at the photo. This time, it was Ian's father who took a deep breath and passed a hand over his eyes.

"Thank you so much, son," he said.

"This means everything to us, Zach," Mary said. "To see him happy doing what he loved. What the good Lord called Ian to do."

Zach pondered Mary's words for moments. What the good Lord called him to do. His gaze fell on Emma and his heart ached for all the times he had failed her and the twins.

It was a moment of stark conviction and self-examination.

When Zach and Emma and the girls were settled back in the cab of the truck, he leaned against the headrest and closed his eyes for a moment.

"I'm so sorry for all you had to go through, Zach," Emma whispered. "I didn't realize how difficult the last year has been. I shouldn't have gotten on your case when you arrived at the ranch."

"I don't matter. Those folks—they're the ones who gave all."

A long silence stretched between them. The only sound was Rachel and Elizabeth murmuring in the back seat.

"Emma, that was really generous of you back there, inviting them to the ranch," Zach finally said.

"Generous? I'm sharing all that God has freely given Big Heart Ranch. That's a gift that has nothing to do with me."

He reached across the truck, pushed her hair back and pressed his lips to her forehead. Emma's eyes rounded wide. "You're a good woman, Emma. I'm sorry I wasn't there for you and the girls. I won't make that mistake again."

A cool autumn breeze, bringing the scent of crushed leaves and sweet-mulched earth, whispered as it passed through the open window of the truck. Zach started the engine. In that moment, he began to understand why the Lord had sent him to Big Heart Ranch. His duty was no longer to his country, but it was to Emma and his brother's children. How he'd fulfill that duty when his plans had him leaving in a few short weeks was the puzzle he'd need to figure out.

Emma parked the ute and got out. She pulled the keys from the little utility vehicle and turned around, her gaze taking in the pretty lights on the gazebo. Zach certainly had done a nice job. Green garland was draped in elegant loops along the top, and a huge wreath with a red bow hung from the front of the roof.

Hmm. Mick said Zach was here, but she didn't see any sign of him except a toolbox and a ladder. "Hello?" she called.

"Up here."

She craned her neck and spotted Zach wedged between the rafters of the gazebo. "What are you doing?"

"What's it look like I'm doing?"

"I'm not sure."

"There are some broken boards in the ceiling. I noticed them when we hung that big wreath from the roof."

"Why didn't you mention this when we talked?"

He shrugged. "Nothing I can't handle."

"Well, then. Thank you."

"It's my job. I'm on Team Emma."

"Team Emma." She sighed, then sat down on the steps and pulled her hoodie close around her.

There was a definite nip in the air today. Fall was fast becoming winter.

"Why are you here?" he asked.

"I need a favor. Team Emma is having problems."

"Uh-oh. I'll be right down."

"No. It can wait. I don't want to interrupt you."

"Stay right there. I'm coming down."

"Please, be careful."

His foot hit the last step and sounded with a thud on the floor of the gazebo. Zach met her gaze through the rungs of the ladder. "I'm trained to be careful."

He dropped a hammer into a toolbox and removed his tool belt, then eased down to the gazebo steps next to her, his left leg stretched out.

The plaid flannel shirt he wore over a navy T-shirt was a very good look. If she was noticing. She tried not to.

Zach smelled of shaved wood and hard work. Not an unappealing scent, either. Emma inched away. After yesterday, she was even more unsettled about their relationship. He'd shared more in the last few days than he had in all the years she'd known him, even when they were kids. Yesterday was especially telling and confusing.

Her bitterness about his not keeping in touch was fading as she realized all he'd been through in the last twelve months.

"Shoot," Zach said.

"Huh?" She raised her head.

"You okay?" he asked.

"Yes. Of course. Lots on my mind."

"You needed a favor?" He said the words slowly.

"Oh, yes. That's right. Feel free to say no," she began.

"I always feel free to say no."

"The manger and stall for the live nativity are in pieces. They simply fell apart during rehearsal this morning. Apparently, they had been stored in the supply barn loft last year and the roof leaked. The whole thing is a mess of rotting wood. We set it up and it promptly collapsed. The three wise men have splinters in untoward places."

Zach slapped his thigh and started laughing.

"The live nativity is really not a laughing matter."

He cleared his throat. "You want me to build a new stall and manger before next Thursday?"

"Yes, please." He was silent for a few moments, and Emma prayed he would be agreeable to her plan.

"We need supplies."

Emma perked up. "I called the hardware store in Timber and they have everything set aside for us. All we have to do is pick it up."

"And build it."

"And build it." Emma resisted a sigh, hoping to keep the optimism flowing. She gave him five more seconds to consider her plan. "What time do you want to go to town?"

"I can go myself."

"I'd like to buy you lunch to thank you for all you've done to help with the Holiday Roundup."

"Emma, that's not necessary. If anything, I should be thanking you for going with me to the Clarks'."

"Okay, you can buy."

Zach blinked, then started laughing. "Well played."

She stood and curtsied. "Thank you."

"I'll meet you at the truck in twenty minutes. I need to put these tools away."

A half hour later, as they drove straight through the heart of downtown Timber, Emma could barely contain her excitement.

"Look," she said. "They've put the flags up."

"You're leaving nose prints on my window," Zach observed.

"I am not." She pointed to the decorative flags flapping in the breeze. "Ooh, they even have snowflake flags this year."

"Flags? What flags are you talking about?"

"Holiday flags on the light posts. Come on, Zach. You lived in this town. They've been putting up holiday flags in Timber since forever."

"No, I lived in a one-bedroom apartment in Tulsa with my mother. I only visited Camelot when the queen deemed it was helpful to her self-serving cause."

Emma sighed. Two brothers and their lives were so vastly different. "Oh, Zach. I'm sorry."

He held up a hand. "Pity is not necessary. I'm explaining why my holiday perspective is nothing like yours."

"Have you considered embracing a new perspective?" she asked. "I'd be delighted to assist with planning and implementation."

"You launched that operation the day I hit Big Heart Ranch."

"You think?" Emma smiled as her gaze swept across the town where volunteers were decorating the giant Christmas tree at the town square park. "You know, it was twenty-five years ago this December that Lucy, Travis and I were pulled out of foster care by our mother's cousin. The first thing we saw was downtown Timber, decorated for the holidays." She grinned. "I was almost five. I will never forget sitting in the back seat of her 1967 wood-paneled Ford station wagon and seeing all the lights of town for the very first time. She parked right along this part of Main Street and we were beneath one of those flags. I was mesmerized. That was when I fell in love with Christmas."

"You remembered that it was a '67 Ford?"

She turned to him. "That was your takeaway from my story?"

Zach shrugged. "Just asking."

"Yes. I remember because she kept that car until she died."

He grimaced. "Sorry. I guess that does explain the whole Christmas overdosing thing."

"I do not overdose. I'm simply enthusiastic."

Zach pulled the truck into a parking spot and Emma unlatched her seat belt. Cold air kissed her face when she stepped out of the vehicle. Temperatures were dropping. Fast. "Brr." She reached back in the truck for her red wool coat.

"What's your rush?" Zach said. He slid his arms into a denim jacket and joined her on the sidewalk.

"Oh, come on. Hurry up, slowpoke."

Zach caught up easily and even with a limp in his step, his long strides equaled six of hers. When they passed the post office, the door swung open, nearly knocking her to the ground. "Oomph."

Warm hands were around her, pulling her close. "You okay, Em?" Zach breathed in her hair.

"Yes. Yes. I believe so." Except for his warm breath on her face, and the heart palpations, yes, she was perfectly fine.

"Sorry, ma'am," the cowboy who had nearly mowed her down said.

"Next time you might want to look before you let that bronc out of the shoot," Zach said.

The cowboy pushed his Stetson to the back of

his head as his gaze moved up Zach's six-foot-five-inch linebacker frame, eyes widening. "Yes, sir. I will."

"I'm fine, Zach," Emma said, straightening her coat.

"Let's be on the safe side." He tucked her hand into the crook of his arm as they continued down the street.

The gesture left Emma near speechless. Zach was being chivalrous, she reminded herself. Former navy SEAL. It came with the territory. She couldn't read anything into it, no matter how nice it felt to be in his arms.

"Think we might get to the diner today?" Zach asked when Emma stopped to examine every single merchant's decorated display window.

"Oh, don't be a bah humbug. I'm going to be swamped pretty soon. This is my last chance to enjoy the decorations."

"Hey, you're the one who got me hungry for the diner's chicken and biscuits." He glanced at his watch. "It's going to be dinner by the time we get there."

Emma stopped, tugged her arm free from Zach and planted her feet in front of the window of the Timber Jewelry Store. "This must be savored."

A silvery-white Christmas tree trimmed with pearl necklace garlands filled the window. The effervescent branches sparkled as the tree slowly twirled around and around like an elegant ballerina. Christmas watches were nestled in the tree's white velvet skirt, along with silver snowflake glitter.

"Oh, look at the watches," Emma murmured.

"All I want for Christmas is a kitschy watch?" he said from behind her.

She turned and met his cynical gaze. "Exactly. The one with the red band and faux-jewel Christmas tree on the face. What fun!"

"Fun. Right." Zach shivered. "You notice it's getting cold out here?"

Emma glanced up at the low-hanging gray clouds covering the sky. "Snow clouds." She took a deep breath and smiled. "It even smells like snow."

"Snow is going to make chores a lot less enjoyable."

"You need a lined barn coat and a hat. You're a full-fledged cowboy again."

"You know, I'm thinking that a good cup of coffee would warm me up."

She hooked her arm in his and pretended to drag him along to the diner.

Pretending. That's what this was. *Right?*

When they got to the diner, the door opened in front of them. This time Emma stepped out of the way.

"Emma?"

She looked up into the smiling face of Beau Randall, a potential RangePro client.

"How are you, Beau?" She turned to Zach. "Beau, this is Zach Norman."

Both men sized each other up. Zach stood towering over the tall rhinestone cowboy with the Hollywood smile and fancy leather jacket, looking none too happy about the situation.

"Norman? Related to Emma?" Beau asked.

"By marriage" was Zach's curt reply.

Beau nodded in dismissal and turned to Emma. "I've been talking to your sales rep, but when am I going to have the CEO of RangePro come out to my ranch and court me properly?"

"You know, Zach is—" Emma paused when Zach put a hand on her arm. She cleared her throat. "Well, Beau, if that's what you want, I can make that happen."

"Terrific. Call my office after the Thanksgiving holiday and we can schedule a meeting. Maybe have lunch at the house." He turned to Zach. "Nice to meet you."

Zach offered the other man a slow nothing of a nod, his eyes narrowed.

"Who is Beau Randall?" Zach asked once their server led them to a booth next to the window.

"A very rich man whose current hobby is dabbling in cattle ranching. He has a huge operation."

"Rich how?"

"Some computer software thing. Built the company from scratch, and then sold it for a small fortune. Apparently, he acquires and sells software companies for a living now." She gestured with a hand. "Picking up his account would be huge for RangePro."

When Zach grunted a response, she turned to look at him. Clearly, something about Beau Randall didn't sit well with him.

"Why didn't you want me to tell him you also own RangePro?" Emma asked.

"Beau Randall doesn't need to know right now." Zach took her coat and hung it on the hook outside the booth. Sitting down, he picked up the menu and fiddled with the pages. "How much are you involved in the day-to-day operations of RangePro?" he asked.

"Steve hired and trained the tech support guy who takes calls from home and troubleshoots. I don't do very much on the software side. I have conference calls weekly with the technician and my sales guys."

"You put out fires."

"Basically, and I'm the face of the company when necessary." She sighed. "And despite my lack of know-how, business is booming."

"Eventually the software will need to be upgraded. What then?"

"I suppose I'll hire someone to do that."

"Proprietary software. It won't be cheap."

"I'm thinking Belgian waffles with whipped cream and a side of sausage," she replied. "They'll do breakfast any time of the day here."

"Emma?"

"Hmm?"

"Come on, Emma, I thought you wanted to talk about RangePro."

"I do." She paused. "I thought I did. But not today." Emma released a breath and played with the Thanksgiving turkey candle nestled next to a small ceramic Santa sitting on the table. "This is not going to end well. It never does, and I'm so enjoying the day."

"Conversation. That's all."

She met his intense gaze and sighed. "I'm listening."

"What's the real reason you don't want to sell RangePro?"

"You aren't going to understand."

"Give me a chance. I'm starting to understand a lot of things since I arrived at Big Heart."

"When I was put in foster care, everything that belonged to my parents was tossed away. The house was emptied." She looked up at him and swallowed. "Every single thing was gone. Their life was erased. I'm afraid that by the time the girls grow up, their father won't even be a memory. Getting rid of RangePro is like getting rid of him." She wrapped her hands tightly around the ceramic Santa. "I can't do that. I can't."

"Hey, hey, relax."

When Zach put his hand over hers, she froze and met his concerned gaze.

"You're right," he said. "Let's change the subject."

Emma nodded and slipped her hand away. She couldn't think when he touched her.

Zach leaned across the table. "I want you to know that I believe there's a solution out there, and I'm just the guy to find it."

"In the meantime, will you go out to Beau Randall's ranch with me?" she asked.

"To let you show me how RangePro works? I could do that at Big Heart Ranch."

"Yes, but Beau is more likely to sign a contract if both owners of the company come out to woo him. The guy is all ego."

"I'm not wooing any rich venture capitalist slash part-time rancher." He scoffed. "He's not even from Oklahoma."

Emma smiled at the disdain in his voice. "You never know, it might get you one step closer to finding a solution to our dilemma."

He made a low rumbling sound. "You really ought to think about running for office."

"Politics? Me?"

"Emma, you're slicker than a boiled onion."

"Oh, you flatterer." She laughed. "And where did you get that phrase from?"

"Who do you think? Dutch." He folded his

menu. "I'll go to Randall's spread with you, but only because I don't want you alone with that guy."

She smiled up at him. "Thank you, Zach."

He shook his head and offered a roll of his eyes.

Driving to the Randall Ranch would be much less stressful with Zach around. Emma blinked. When had she transitioned to being comfortable in Zach's company? It seemed only yesterday things were tense between them. Now she not only liked him around, she realized that she actually looked forward to his presence.

That might very well be a mistake because Zach Norman wouldn't be around much longer.

Chapter Eight

Zach tugged open the door to the chow hall against the brisk wind and stopped just inside, slightly stunned by the scene before him. The Big Heart Ranch staff and children filled the room for the Thanksgiving celebration. This gathering was bigger than the Christmas party of weeks before, no doubt because there was a surplus of children. All ages and sizes.

Delicious food aromas mingling with whispers of excitement drifted to him, confirming that today was special. A meal of thanks followed by the lights-on ceremony. Anticipation sizzled in the room as folks chatted, laughed and hugged each other. Though the room was packed, nobody seemed to care.

The only easy day was yesterday.

The words from his training days failed to dispel the strong desire to quietly step back and retreat out the door to safer ground. Alone. There was safety in alone.

He was trained for one-on-one, not this crowd. Zach surveyed the landscape and released a pained breath.

Before he had a chance to act on a primal urge to bail, his little niece Rachel slammed into him and wrapped her arms tightly around his kneecaps in a mini bear hug. "Unca Zach!"

His heartstrings were yanked at the simple words.

"Rachel!" he returned with a grin.

She giggled with delight at his animated response.

Reaching down, he scooped her up in his arms and moved his grocery store shopping sack to the other hand.

"Your mommy dresses you in holiday cheer, doesn't she?" Zach asked Rachel as he straightened her little red sweater.

She nodded and tucked her head under his chin.

After four weeks, he no longer required the color-coding handicap. He could easily tell Rachel and Elizabeth apart. The soft inflections in their toddler voices, the mannerisms. Rachel lit up when she saw him and jumped into his arms without hesitation while Elizabeth stood back assessing before she committed.

"How's my girl?" he asked.

"Hungy. I wanna eat."

"Okay, let's get my girl food."

Across the room, Emma turned as though she sensed his presence. Elizabeth was in her arms in a matching purple sweater. Emma's eyes widened and though Zach didn't have a clue about women, when a slow sweet smile touched her lips it sure seemed like she was glad to see him.

Emma's smile was lethal. It knocked his heart sideways every time. Like a magnet, he felt the irresistible pull and started across the room toward her.

Then Tripp Walker stepped in his way.

"Got a minute?" the taciturn horse manager asked in his slow, measured voice.

Though about fifty pounds lighter, Tripp was the only person at the ranch who, at six foot five, stood eye to eye with Zach. The horse whisperer, as everyone called him, stared with intensity.

"Sure, Tripp," Zach replied, his gaze drifting back to Emma.

"I'd like to get you on board to train the boys for the Big Heart Rodeo competition."

"The summer one?"

Tripp nodded.

"Isn't that Travis's territory?"

"Some. Mostly he's too busy." Tripp shook his head. "Things haven't been the same since he went and fell in love."

"Yeah, I'm washing my hands constantly, praying it isn't contagious."

The corner of Tripp's mouth pulled into a whisper of a smile. "I think it might be too late for you," he murmured.

Zach blinked at the comment, but let it pass. "You think I'm qualified?"

Tripp gave a nod of acknowledgment. "The boys like and respect you. That's enough of a qualification for me, right there."

"Ah, thanks. When does training start?" he asked.

"Full-time in the spring. But I'm going to talk to Lucy about renting hours at the indoor arena in Timber right after the holidays."

"You know I'm only here until January, right?"

"You sure about that?" Tripp asked.

"Well, yeah I'm sure. Unless you know something I don't."

Tripp's gaze followed his across the room to the spot where Emma stood chatting with Pastor Parr and his mother. "No. I believe we both have the same information," he murmured.

Zach offered an awkward laugh at the words. "Can I get back to you?"

"Sure thing."

Zach stood there for a moment, confused by the exchange.

"Food, Unca Zach," Rachel reminded him.

"Yeah. I'm on it, sweetie."

Lucy Maxwell Harris was the next to step in his path. "Zach, so good to see you."

"Thanks, Lucy. How are you doing?"

She folded both hands serenely on top of her abdomen. "Fine. I'm getting fat and lazy, lying around, but only a few more weeks left." Lucy smiled and reached for the grocery bag on his arm. "Here, let me take that from you."

"It's just store-bought chips and dip. Dutch said I had to bring something if I want pie. Trouble is, I don't cook."

"Dutch said that, did he? And did he mention that he only brings his appetite?"

Zach rubbed his chin. "You know, that old wrangler keeps pulling one over on me and I never even see it coming."

"You're the new guy, that's why. Stick around and come spring we'll be bringing a few new wranglers in and you'll be considered the old guy."

"I'm only here a few more weeks myself."

"I can't see you leaving your nieces." Lucy cocked her head and smiled at Rachel in his arms. "No. Not going to happen."

He opened his mouth to respond when Emma joined them with Elizabeth.

"Zach, you made it." She looked from Lucy back to him. "Is my sister giving you a hard time?"

"Me? Never." Lucy smiled serenely. "Come

on, girls, let's get you something to eat while Mommy visits with Uncle Zach."

"Down," Rachel demanded.

Zach released her. "Apparently I'm only number two in her life."

Emma put Elizabeth on the ground and both girls took Lucy's hands. "Never stand between a Maxwell and a meal," Lucy said.

"That is so not true," Emma said.

"Sure it is," Lucy said. "Why do you think I married Jack? Because he cooks better than I do." She winked and led the twins toward the long buffet table of platters and serving dishes.

"Speaking of food," Zach said. "What did the midnight baker bring?"

"I made a pumpkin roll, and then I baked chocolate chip cookies." She smiled. "Those were made in your honor."

"How did you fit baking into your schedule? I know for a fact you were out directing those tree trucks that arrived way too late last night. When did you sleep?"

"We have very long and ugly winters here, punctuated by lots of ice storms. I can sleep after the holidays are over."

"That's how you get run-down," Zach said.

"No. I never get sick."

"Famous last words."

She looked at him. "How did you know about the trucks anyhow?"

"I did a walk-through and also checked on the stall and manger."

"Everything is in order?"

"I got the wise men seal of approval."

Emma smiled. "I don't know what we would have done if you hadn't agreed to help with the roundup." She paused. "Zach, you really have saved the day."

"We haven't even turned the lights on and it's four weeks until Christmas. Plenty of time for me to mess things up."

She shook her head and offered a small gasp. "Don't even whisper such a thing. Your presence here has been a blessing."

"Ever notice you tend to embellish?"

"Not this time." She turned toward the window and her eyes lit up. "Look, the Clarks are here."

Zach glanced through the floor-to-ceiling glass windows of the cafeteria in time to see Mary and Joe Clark getting out of their car. He walked to the door and held it open when they approached.

"So glad you could make it," Emma said.

While Zach stood by, uncertain of the protocol, Emma ushered the couple in. She had a servant's heart and her welcoming hug was effortless and genuine.

"Oh, thank you, dear. You make me feel like family."

"Good. That's what we want," Emma returned.

Mary smiled and held up a plastic-covered

cake plate for all to see and handed it to Emma. "I brought dessert."

"That looks like it might be a hummingbird cake," Emma said.

"Yes. Normally I only make one or two a year, but it's not every day we're invited to Big Heart Ranch."

"We may have to hide it," Emma said with a mischievous grin.

Joe smiled. "I like how you think."

Mary tugged off her gloves and glanced around. "Where are the twins?"

"They're across the room with my sister," Emma said. "Come on, let's find them and I'll introduce you to the family and friends of Big Heart Ranch."

Emma paused and placed a hand on Zach's arm. "The boys have arrived."

"Which boys?" he asked.

"I invited Benjie and Mick as our special guests. Normally, they'd have Thanksgiving at their ranch house."

"Emma, that was really nice of you."

She nodded toward the door. "Do you want to welcome them?"

"Sure. Go ahead. I've got this."

She met his gaze. "Save a few seats for me and the girls at your table. Okay?"

"Yes, ma'am."

Benjie and Mick pushed open the door and

glanced around nervously. Both boys wore dress shirts and slacks under their winter coats. Mick's dark hair had been combed into order, and Benjie's wild curls were slicked back.

"Hey, guys," Zach said.

"Mr. Zach," both said in unison. Relief covered their faces. "You invited us to dinner?"

"Technically, it was Miss Emma." He cocked his head toward the tables. "After dinner, we're going to watch lights-on."

"We can go with you?" Mick asked, eyes shining.

"Sure. You did a lot of the work, so you get a front seat."

Zach turned and assessed the buffet line. "Come on, let's go find some hors d'oeuvres. The smell of all those Crock-Pots simmering is making my stomach grumble."

"What's an or-derve?" Mick asked.

"Snacks before the big dinner spread," Zach explained.

"I'm in," Benjie said with a high five to his brother.

"Oh, yeah," Mick echoed.

It was only a short time later that Lucy tapped on a microphone and invited everyone to find a seat as they prepared to offer thanks. Emma pulled Rachel's and Elizabeth's high chairs up to the end of one of the long tables, right next to Zach. Then she slid into the chair beside him.

Benjie and Mick sat across from them next to Joe and Mary.

"Let's bow our heads while Pastor Parr offers a prayer of thanksgiving for the staff and their families," Lucy continued.

When Emma slipped her small hand into his, Zach froze. He took Rachel's chubby fingers and glanced around the table, his gaze sweeping the silent room, his heart humbled.

"Lord, on this special day of thanks we thank You for Your bountiful and endless goodness and for Your many blessings. Thank You, for each man, woman and child of Big Heart Ranch. Help us to set our eyes and our hearts on You every day. Renew us and fill us with Your peace and joy. We give You praise and thanks and ask You to bless this meal and this time of fellowship. Amen."

A soft and sincere choir of amen echoed across the room.

Emma squeezed Zach's hand before she released it. He swallowed hard against the unfamiliar emotions crowding him. There was so much to be thankful for today. Family and friends, all in one place and grateful to have him present.

He looked up and met the eager faces of Mick and Benjie. The hopeful smiles of Joe and Mary. To his left, Rachel and Elizabeth beamed like little queens reigning over the table. Zach dared to meet Emma's gaze, turned toward him.

"Does it get any better than this?" she murmured.

"I don't see how it could," he returned.

How was he going to give all this up come January? His chest hurt with the thought and he rubbed a fist against his sternum. Leaving would be too cruel to consider.

You don't have to.

The words filled his head and shook him to his core. Did he dare consider staying on at Big Heart Ranch? Could there truly be a forever place for him here?

Once again, his gaze landed on Emma. He'd protected his heart for far too long. It was ready to burst with tenderness for Emma and the girls. Was there room in her heart for another?

He had four weeks. A lot could happen in a month.

"Ten. Nine. Eight. Seven. Six. Five. Four. Three. Two. One. Lights on!"

Emma yelled right along with the rest of the entire staff and children of Big Heart Ranch as the lights-on ceremony began.

Applause erupted and "oohs" and "aahs" went up when the lights of Big Heart Ranch came on, illuminating not only the sky, but the entire trail with a brilliant glow.

"Zach, look at those LED lights of yours," Emma said. "They're so bright."

"I did okay, huh?" Zach whispered. He held a sleeping Rachel in his arms and stood next to Emma, who held Elizabeth.

She reached over and tugged the fleece covering over Rachel snug around her shoulders. "Yes. You did," she said. "Look around you. This is the start of all that is amazing and wondrous about the Christmas season and you, Zach Norman, made it happen."

"You're going to ruin my street cred as a Scrooge."

"Nonsense," Emma returned.

He turned to the boys. "What did you think of our lights, guys?" Zach asked Benjie and Mick.

"That was so cool," Mick said. "And I helped."

"So did I," Benjie chimed in.

"You both did a great job," Emma said. She pointed to the parking lot behind them. "There's your house mother. Time to head home."

"Do we have to? Can't we stay a little longer?" Mick pleaded.

"It's late, Mick, and I know for a fact that you and Benjie have stable duty on Fridays," Zach said.

"We have to feed the horses on a holiday?" Benjie asked, eyes rounding.

"Sure you do. You're assigned a horse every day of the year. Grace doesn't care if it's a holiday. That mare wants her flakes and oats." He patted Mick on the shoulder. "I'm proud of you guys. Now give me a 'yes, sir.'"

"Yes, sir," they echoed.

"Night, boys," Emma said.

"Night, Miss Emma. Mr. Zach," Benjie said.

"Thanks for inviting us to the party," Mick said. He put his arm around his little brother's shoulders and led him toward their house mom.

"Look at that," Emma said. "That's a beautiful sight. You did that, you know."

"Nah, they just grew into each other."

"You're wrong, Zach. You have really made a difference in their lives. You're good at this."

"Good at what?"

"Being a big brother. Being a friend." She looked at Rachel nestled in his arms. "Good at being an uncle."

"Thanks, Emma," he said softly.

Thanks. She should be thanking him. This had been the best Thanksgiving in a long time. As they stood together staring at the lights, bright against the velvet backdrop of the night sky, she offered silent thanksgiving to God.

"Who has first shift with the trees tomorrow?" Zach asked.

"You had to mention tomorrow. That would be

Travis and AJ. Which means the rest of us will be moving the herd and riding the fence line."

"Let's hope the weather holds," Zach said.

"A few snowflakes would be nice," Emma said. "I'd like a white Christmas."

"Sure, everyone likes snow until they're standing knee-deep in a drift trying to move a stubborn heifer."

Emma chuckled. "I'm going to put that right out of my mind."

"We're gonna need some volunteers to practice the carriage rides, folks," Dutch announced as he moved through the crowd. "It's a fine night for a little stargazing."

"A cold night, you mean," someone called out.

From the direction of the stables, four black-and-white horse-drawn carriages approached with a clip-clop of hooves and a jingle of bells hanging from the horses' tack.

Emma moved through the crowd to Joe and Mary Clark. "Do you two want to take a ride? The carriages have blankets."

"What do you say, Joseph?" Mary looked to her husband.

"Sure." He winked at his wife. "A carriage ride with a beautiful woman. That's a no-brainer."

"Oh, Emma, you've certainly made this a night to remember," Mary said as she took Joe's hand.

"I'm glad you've had fun."

"I have, and it's good to see you and Zach so happy."

"Zach?"

"He's a keeper, you know," Mary whispered.

"Pardon me?"

"Zach. That young fellow is over the moon in love with you and your girls."

Emma frowned and glanced down at Elizabeth, still sleeping in her arms. "Oh, yes, he's crazy about his nieces."

"Their momma, too, dear. But then you knew that, didn't you?" She gave Emma a hug before her husband led her to the carriage.

"I, um..." Emma stood staring after the couple.

"Let me take the girls home tonight."

"Hmm?" Emma turned at her sister's voice.

"You deserve a break. Look at all you and Zach have done. The roundup is going to be amazing."

"Lucy, you're pregnant and you have triplets. Get serious." As they spoke, the Harris triplets Dub, Ann and Eva played tag on the grass outside the chow hall.

"It's bedtime for those three," Lucy said. "The twins are already conked out. I'll put your girls in the guest room and turn on the baby monitor. No big deal."

Jack Harris appeared at his wife's side and took Elizabeth from Emma's arms. "You know better than to argue with Lucy. Take a ride with the rest of them."

"The rest of them?"

"With Zach and AJ and Travis." He nodded to the two open carriages that Dutch held for them.

"You gonna take all day?" Dutch asked when he got Travis and AJ settled.

"I don't think this is such a good idea," Emma murmured, with a questioning glance at Zach.

"Where's your Christmas spirit?" Zach challenged with a wink.

Lucy reached over and took Rachel from Zach. "We didn't ask you."

"Come on, Emma," Zach persisted. "Let's take a ride and see your hard work up close."

"I would like to see the rest of the trail," she murmured. It was the whole sitting next to Zach, in the close confines of the carriage thing that concerned her.

"There you go," he said.

Emma followed him to the carriage where Dutch pulled out a stool. She placed her hand in Zach's and stepped inside.

"Your knee..."

"I'm fine," Zach said as he slowly climbed in beside her.

"So where do these carriages come from?" he asked as he pulled the blanket from between them and carefully tucked the plaid wool around Emma and himself.

"One of our locals. He rents them to us half price. We get four for the price of two. Did you notice the banner advertisement on the side? Oklahoma Livery. He provides the horses and we provide the drivers."

"No moon tonight. Dark as a pocket overhead," Dutch called from the driver's seat.

"Having fun, Dutch?" Zach called.

"No, we're not done. Barely started." He lifted the reins and clicked his tongue.

Emma bit her lip. "He can't hear us over the clopping of the horses and the jangling of the sleigh bells."

"Which isn't a bad thing," Zach said.

"Look," Emma said. "Bell ringers in the gazebo."

Dutch slowed the buggy as the melodic ding-dong of chiming bells rang out "Silent Night."

"Giddap," Dutch said when the music ended. They stopped again down the road in front of the pond, where costumed carolers stood on a covered stage singing mash-ups of Christmas songs.

"The lights look pretty reflected off the water," Emma said. "You did such an amazing job."

"I only hung them, Emma. You handed me a display map that a ten-year-old could follow." He laughed. "Oh, wait, he did."

Emma shivered and pulled the blanket up.

"Cold?" Zach asked. His breath came out in cloudy puffs.

"Maybe a bit," she returned hesitantly.

Zach nodded to the sky as his arm came around her. "It's starting to snow."

"Look, it's snowing," Dutch called over his shoulder.

Around them flakes danced in the air as if to the music. Weightless, they swirled, twirled and pirouetted through the sky and to the ground.

"Well, ain't that just pretty?" Dutch continued.

"Beautiful," Emma said.

"Sure hope that live nativity has the heater set up or those wise men are gonna freeze their royal tootsies off," Dutch said with a laugh.

"I haven't seen snow in years," Zach murmured.

"Didn't you miss all this?"

"Emma, missing began years ago. Every single time I was picked up by mother I missed something."

"Maybe you're getting a second chance. An opportunity to start over."

"Could be."

Once again, Dutch stopped the carriage. This time outside the live nativity.

"Is that a real baby?" Zach asked.

"In case you're wondering, that's not a real baby," Dutch called from his perch.

Emma choked on a laugh.

From inside the stall, above the manger, a radiant beam of light shone through the roof into the deep purple and black night.

"It's like a star," Emma said. "How did they do that?"

"*They* might have had a little help," Zach said.

"Oh, Zach, it's perfect. Absolutely perfect."

One of the wise men stepped forward and began to speak. "'For unto us a child is born, unto us a son is given, and the government shall be upon his shoulder: and his name shall be called Wonderful, Counsellor, The mighty God, The everlasting Father, The Prince of Peace.'"

Emma's heart tripped at the power and significance of the words from the King James Bible.

When Zach's arm tightened around her it seemed right and natural.

Could there be a more perfect night than this? A night of thanks for today and hope for tomorrow.

Chapter Nine

"This was your doing, wasn't it?" Zach said. He grunted and hauled another bale of hay onto the flatbed of the two-ton ranch truck, glaring at the steadily falling curtain of snow. Two hours and the precipitation hadn't let up. Mother Nature was determined to cover Big Heart Ranch in snow.

"Me?" Emma laughed at his observation as she shoved wet strands of hair back from her face and tugged a black wool beanie over her ears. She used two gloved hands to push the bale of hay from the front, toward the cab.

"You were hoping for snow for the holidays," Zach reminded her.

"I'm pretty certain that I never actually specified an amount. My order was for a few dazzling flakes. Something like a Bing Crosby and Danny Kaye movie was my plan. Then I could dance and sing around the pine tree in my front yard while wearing my red velvet dress and fur muff. You know, like Rosemary Clooney."

"Who?"

Emma slapped a gloved hand to her forehead. "I have my work cut out for me with you," she said. "Talk about Christmas challenged. There's a holiday movie marathon in your near future, Zach."

"Great and in the meantime, could you pull whatever strings you have and get the snow to stop?"

She looked at the sky with pure delight and raised a gloved hand to catch flakes that swirled down, blanketing everything in white. "This is more than I requested and it came out of nowhere. Blame the weatherman. He submitted the wrong snow order."

Zach cleared his throat. "Ready?" he asked with a nod toward the bed of the truck.

She stepped out of the way and he tossed another bale in. Was it his imagination, or were the bales getting heavier? He used to be at peak condition. What happened? Three surgeries and a certain someone's baking. That's what. He'd gotten used to the treats Emma regularly offered the wranglers.

Zach did a double take when Emma picked up the bale he had just added to the truck and piled it on another. The pint-size Wonder Woman was showing him up.

When she stepped aside, he took a deep breath, sucked in his gut, braced his feet and tossed another bale onto the truck in one swift movement. Neat trick, except he nearly undid the last surgical procedure on his knee in the process. He stumbled backward two steps and caught himself.

"Maybe you should slow down," Emma said.

"Naw. I got this." He dusted off his hands attempting to salvage his ego. "What were you saying?"

"I said that we had great weather for fall calving and for getting the Holiday Roundup decorations up," she said. "I'm grateful for that. This is a minor nuisance."

"Freezing temperatures and blinding snow is a minor nuisance." Zach frowned. "Is there anything you can't put a spin on?"

She stopped and considered his words. "Probably not."

"I appreciate your honesty."

Emma pushed on the hay. "Life is all about choices, Zach. I choose to be happy."

"Duly noted."

"Oh, come on. Think of all the fun we can have tomorrow."

"How's that?"

"If the temperature doesn't drop too much we can take the girls and Benjie and Mick and the triplets up to the hill behind the supply barn and go sledding. Build snowmen and practice our snow angels."

"Yeah, okay, I concede that sledding with kids might be fun, but I'm having a hard time finding joy in that thought when I'm wet and cold." Zach straightened and stretched his back.

"If you'd stop dressing like a California boy, it might help." She peered over the edge of the truck. "For starters, you've got a denim jacket on and I wouldn't be surprised if you were wearing flip-flops."

"Not today." Zach laughed. "You know, right about now, AJ and Travis are sitting in a trailer with a nice warm heater selling trees and smiling because we got herd duty."

"Their time will come," she said. "You and I are assigned the Christmas tree sales on Saturday."

"I'll bring the hot chocolate," Zach said.

Emma straightened and grinned. "Okay, and I'll bring my chocolate muffins."

"Best offer I've had all day. Now I can't wait for Saturday."

Was it his imagination or did Emma's face pink at his words?

He nodded toward the hay. "How's it looking?"

"One more and we're full."

"How come Travis doesn't have a bale processor?" He narrowed his gaze. "Maybe I should share my views on redundancy with him."

"You're a rancher's son. You should know that a rancher's life is nothing but redundancy." Emma laughed.

"And the baler?"

"Maybe someday. For now, we aren't even producing and baling our own hay at Big Heart. The operation is less than two years old and Travis only hired AJ last spring."

"This is way too much work for an out-of-shape former navy SEAL."

"It could be worse. Travis is split calving right now. So the herd isn't as big as it could be." Emma sat down on the truck bed and dangled her boots over the edge. "I'm exhausted." She closed her eyes and put her head against a bale of hay.

Zach leaned against the truck and looked out at the fields where every inch of grass not covered by snow was stiff with frost. "Good to know I'm not alone."

Emma chuckled. "Those cows complained all the way to the south pasture, didn't they?"

"First snow of the year. They're as annoyed as we are."

"I tried to explain to them that there was protection from the wind in the south pasture, but they kept bellowing." She sighed. "Now we have to feed them. They're exactly like my children. Eat, sleep, eliminate and complain."

"I guess we do have it easy today. No drifts yet." He glanced at Emma, still tucked back against the bale of hay with her eyes closed. Her breathing had become even and regular.

The youngest Maxwell was beautiful, more so with a dusting of snowflakes. Dark hair framed the perfectly oval face. There was no one more beautiful inside and out than Emma. The pureness of her heart radiated when she smiled.

And she was going to be spitting nails in a minute.

Zach reached down, balled up snow in his glove and aimed for the hay bale next to her. The snowball hit and spattered.

"Hey!" Wild-eyed, she jumped to attention.

"Wake up, Miss Christmas. We aren't done yet and I'd like to finish before it gets dark."

"I was only resting my eyes." Emma stood and stretched.

She took a long look at the pasture. "No picture can capture the beauty of the land. We were blessed when we were given all of this."

"I agree. Now quit waxing poetic and let's get moving so we can admire the beauty of the land from the house, sipping hot chocolate in front of a fire."

"You're a slave driver. Don't you ever wax poetic?"

He shrugged but was silent. *Only when I'm looking at you, Emma.*

"Here we go," Zach said, reaching for a bale. "Last one."

Emma guided it into place and turned to him. "Do you really mind being out here?" She cocked her head and met his gaze. "Steve hated ranch life. He was happiest behind his computer working away."

"I'm nothing like my brother. I'm guessing you figured that out a long time ago."

She offered a solemn nod.

"And for the record, I'm giving you a hard time because I can." He let a small smile slip past his lips. "I wouldn't have signed up for wrangler duty if I minded. This is almost as much fun as swimming in subzero temperatures with my SEAL team buddies."

"You said the word *fun*."

"So I did." He smiled. "Come on, let me help you down. We need to finish Big Heart Ranch cattle Meals on Wheels and get you home to the twins."

Emma stepped closer to the edge of the flatbed and he put his hands around her waist through her thick barn coat. As if in slow motion, he lifted her through the air and eased her down to the ground. She weighed less than a bag of oats.

When he set her down, she stared up at him, the brown eyes wide and assessing. "You have snow in your hair," she said softly. "I'm going to have to buy you a proper cowboy hat for Christmas."

When she raised her arm to brush away the

flakes, he caught her hand and pressed a kiss to her gloved palm, his eyes never leaving hers. Tucking her hand close between them, Zach was unable to resist lowering his head. It was a slow movement, allowing her the option to step away.

But she didn't.

Zach's lips gently touched Emma's, and the world slipped away for a long moment.

When he released her, Emma remained in the circle of his arms while snow fell from the sky, cocooning them as they stood together.

"I wasn't expecting that," she murmured.

"Pretend it never happened," he said. Because he knew that it shouldn't have.

She met his gaze. Tiny crystals of snow rested on her lashes and cheek. "I mean, I didn't expect to feel so much."

"Emma, stop analyzing." Zach touched a finger to her face to wipe away a crystal.

Then he turned and pulled the keys from his pocket. "Ready?" he asked.

"Yes."

They drove to the pasture in silence. When they got to the paddock, Emma climbed out of the truck and jogged to the fence to open the gate. Zach drove in and she closed it again behind him.

He rolled down his window. "Can you get back up in the bed okay?"

"Sure," she said. Her face revealed nothing. As

usual, Emma put on a smile for the world, hiding what she was thinking and feeling.

"Stomp on the truck bed when they're all dumped out," Zach said. "I'll park it and help you rake out the hay."

It took a quarter of the time to dump the hay as it took to load the truck. When Emma had kicked all the bales to the ground, he stopped the truck and got out. Together they split the bales and loosened the hay. The cattle came running as though they'd heard the supper bell.

Emma leaned on a rake catching her breath and sending clouds of condensation into the air. "We've earned our paycheck today."

"That we have." He tossed his rake in the back of the truck.

For a moment she stared at him, a wistful expression on her face before she turned away.

"Emma. Look at me," he said.

"Hmm?"

"It's going to be okay. It was just a kiss." He didn't believe the words, but he said them anyhow.

"I know," she said with a smile. "It's just that I didn't realize how much I would like it."

Zach jerked back at the unexpected words and he laughed. "Get in the truck, cowgirl. Let's go home."

He was over his head right now and the potential for drowning was real. Time to step back and figure out what his next move was, and whether it would hurt as much as he suspected it would.

"Dutch, do you have time to help me cut a tree?" Emma called from Rodeo's stall.

When there was no response, she looked over the gate. The weathered cowboy turned and stared at her as if she had lost her mind.

"It's colder than a cast-iron commode out there, Miss Emma. And the snow looks like it won't stop neither." He stroked his silver mustache and gave a slow shake of his head. "Cutting a tree in this weather's like trying to put socks on a rooster. Plain makes no sense."

Emma stepped out of the stall, latched the gate and crossed her arms. "This is the warmest day we've had since Thanksgiving and it hasn't snowed since yesterday."

"Tell that to my joints. They ain't what they used to be. I'm not a youngster, you know."

"Fine." She spun around and headed to the tack room. "I'll do it myself."

The cowboy laughed. "Not on my watch. Give me a minute to get my thermals and extra socks on." He paused and glared at her. "You're sure it has to be today, huh?"

"Weather calls for more snow on Friday. Tomorrow we move cattle again. It has to be today. You know I like to get my tree cut before Travis and Lucy."

Fifteen minutes later, the big outer door creaked open and the sound of boots stomping in place echoed into the stables.

"Dutch, is that you? Can you grab the rope?"

"Nope. It's Scrooge," Zach said. "But I grabbed the rope anyhow."

Emma grimaced and gave a wary laugh.

She had been avoiding Zach for a week. He knew it and she knew it. Now she peeked out of Rodeo's stall and prayed that he would go away. Zach Norman had kissed her, and she was more than unopposed to the idea. How was she supposed to process that? She was confused and didn't understand what the rules were for young widows beneath the age of…whatever. The topic had never come up in three years. Could she dare risk the crushing pain of loss again? Especially since Zach was leaving.

"I know you're here, Emma. I can hear you thinking."

"Is there something I can help you with?" Emma peeked out at him again. "Dutch and I are going to cut my Christmas tree."

Zach chuckled as he looped the rope around his shoulder. "Dutch sent me here to help you. He's on his way into Timber in that beat-up truck of his to catch a movie."

"Remind me to put coal in his stocking," Emma muttered. She sighed and grabbed her saddle.

"I'm here, ready and willing. Let me help."

The sound of his footsteps said he was coming closer.

"Oh, that's not necessary," she returned quickly. "I can do it another time. No big deal. Christmas is a long way off."

"Long way off, huh? Since when?" He snorted a laugh. "Emma, are you by chance avoiding me?"

She turned when she realized that he stood outside Rodeo's stall. When her gaze landed on his mouth, Emma blinked and forced herself to stare at his left ear.

"Why would I do that?" she said sweetly.

"I can make an educated guess, but maybe you should tell me." Zach turned around, a puzzled expression on his face. "What are you looking at?"

"Nothing."

"What happened Saturday?" he asked. "We were scheduled to work Christmas tree detail. I brought the hot chocolate, and then I ended up sharing it with Dutch, not you. I got to hear eight hours of nonstop John Wayne trivia and instead of muffins I got teriyaki beef jerky and pork rinds." Zach shuddered. "I'm probably traumatized for life."

Emma sighed, knowing she was in the wrong. "Okay, I apologize for that." She opened the stall, stepped out, and walked up and down the stables, checking beneath every single door.

"Are you even listening to me?" Zach asked.

"Yes. Of course."

"What are you doing?"

"I don't want anyone to know my business. Gossip spreads like a sneeze through a screen door around here."

"Another Dutch-ism if I ever heard one," he mumbled. "It's like the language of the land at Big Heart Ranch."

She put her hands on her hips and slapped her most sincere "I'm the boss" expression on. "Zach, it's not wise for me to fraternize with a fellow employee."

"Okay, yeah. That's good." He chuckled. "I like that. Rule twenty-seven in the Big Heart Ranch employee manual."

Emma frowned. Not only was she out of practice at playing boss, but she was up against a navy SEAL. He was trained in intimidation.

"Is that really the best you can do?" Zach asked.

"I'm being serious."

"Why not just admit you've been avoiding me because I kissed you?" He paused. "You weren't opposed to the kiss at the time, as I recall."

"There were extenuating circumstances. I was exhausted, hungry and sleep deprived."

"Do you want to try it again to be sure? I'm not busy at the moment."

She raised a hand to her lips and stepped back. “No!”

Zach laughed. “Fine by me.”

“Look, I’m sorry you had to spend the day with Dutch, but it seemed a good idea to put a bit of distance between us and the situation.”

“Right. Until clearer heads could prevail.” He was silent for moments, simply looking at her. “It was a kiss. Albeit a very good one. Let’s forget it and move on.”

She brightened at his words. Yes, exactly. It was time to act like a mature adult instead of a teenager.

“I can do that,” she said.

“Terrific. Now, do you mind telling me why you’re cutting a tree when you have a tent full of perfectly good Christmas trees for sale?”

“Memories.”

“You’ll have to explain.”

“It’s one of the few things I remember about my parents. We went to the woods every year and cut down our own tree. I’ve kept the tradition up all my life.”

“I can respect that. Okay, sure. Let’s do it.”

“Are you sure you don’t mind? Though the wind’s eased up, the thermometer’s still sitting at thirty-two.”

“I’ve got a new coat to break in.”

“You do!” She stepped around him, assessing

the dark blue faux shearling-lined barn jacket. "I like it. It looks…"

"Don't say lovely."

"Rugged and handsome." She frowned. "You went all the way into town. Why didn't you get a hat?"

"I went to town for Christmas shopping. The coat was collateral damage when it started snowing again and I figured out my denim jacket wasn't doing the job."

"Christmas shopping! Really? You did?"

"Yeah. Happens to the best of us."

She tamped down her enthusiasm. No need to give him a hard time when he had voluntarily stepped into new territory. "So the hat? You were saying?"

"I tried a few, but…"

"A Stetson or a Resistol?"

"Both. I'm only here two and a half more weeks. Seems like a waste of money to me."

"Two and a half weeks?" She swallowed the words and they settled in her stomach like a cement sandwich. *Two and a half weeks. How could that be?*

"I guess we better pick up our pace. You've hardly gotten any Christmas cheer in yet," she finally said.

"Oh, I'm good. Dutch also made me watch a John Wayne Christmas movie."

"There's a John Wayne Christmas movie?"

"Yeah, it has a tree, presents and everything. I can't recall the name. I dozed off."

"Who knew?" she mused. "All the same, time really is going fast, isn't it?"

"Yeah," he said, his voice low and quiet.

"Two weeks," she murmured again.

"Are we riding to get a tree?" Zach asked.

"Hmm?" She lifted her head, brushing away the disturbing thoughts. "What did you say?"

"Horses?"

"Oh, yes. Much more fun. The snow is light and there isn't any ice yet."

"And you're all about the *f-u-n*."

Emma chuckled. "Now you get it."

"Yeah, right. I've heard that song before. And about the time I memorize the lyrics it'll be time for a new song."

Emma saddled Rodeo and met Zach and Zeus outside. Though the sky was clear and blue and the sun was out, the air remained tight with a dry chill. Rodeo's breath puffed out in vapor clouds as they followed Zach down the trail that ran parallel to the road. The path was clear of snow, and despite the cold, the ride was pleasant. Dutch didn't know what he was missing.

Though truth be told, she'd rather be with Zach. And right there was the problem.

"How far are we going?" he called over his shoulder.

"Not far. The woods across the road from the

pond have a nice selection. We plant a few up here every year since Lucy and Travis also cut down their own. I like to get up here first. A little healthy tree competition."

"Yeah. I saw that one coming." He pointed to the right a few minutes later. "There?"

"Yes," she said. They left the trail and plodded through the snowy pasture to the thicket of trees.

"Virginia pine," Emma said. "Let's walk around and find a good one. I'm not looking for a big tree. Something about my size will be perfect."

Zach dismounted and followed her around the grove of graceful pines, dusted with snow. Their feet crunched on the snow, leaving prints as they walked.

"How about that one?" He pointed to a five-foot tree near the front. "I've got your horse, go take a look."

"You know, I think this is the perfect tree. Hardly any gaps between the branches. Good eye." She pulled the saw in its leather sheath from her saddle.

"I thought I was going to cut it down," Zach said.

"Oh? I'm sorry. I usually do that."

He raised a hand. "Hey, have at it."

Emma removed a few flimsy branches in the way at the base and measured from the ground before she set the blade into position, preparing to saw straight across the trunk. After ten futile minutes of cutting, she stood straight and took a deep breath.

Was it this difficult last year? Surely not. Then again, she'd spent an awful lot of time at her desk the last twelve months.

"Doing okay?" Zach called.

With a glance, Emma noted the massive shoulders and bulk of her companion. What was she thinking? She'd brought a lumberjack with her. Let the man saw the tree.

"Your turn. Please."

"Yes, ma'am." Zach offered a macho grin, handed her the reins and took the saw. Minutes later, he gave a shove, and the pine fell backward.

"Nice work. Why didn't you yell *timber*?"

He shrugged. "I thought you'd laugh."

"We're friends. I'd only laugh with you." Her lips twitched.

"Yeah, like I believe that." He dragged the tree into the clearing. "Got any twine?"

Emma pulled the twine from her saddlebag and tossed it to him. Then she handed over a neatly folded canvas tarp.

"Tarp? That's not how they do it in the movies."

"It's my tree and I want it intact when I get it home."

"Tarp it is." When he finished, he looked up at her. "You want to drag it home with Rodeo?"

"You bagged the wild Christmas tree. I'll give you the honors."

He grinned like a kid. "You know, Emma, that actually was fun."

"I'm glad." She smiled back. "So this whole holiday experience is sort of growing on you?"

"Yeah, I guess it is." He grinned. "Thanks to you."

"That makes me very happy, Zach."

Emma put her boot in the stirrup and took her place in the saddle, ready to ride. She looked away as a courtesy to Zach, who was still clumsy mounting his horse with his stiff knee.

He offered a holler and a raised hand when he was ready, and she cued Rodeo to follow Zach and the Christmas tree. As they got closer to the ranch, he turned in the saddle and winked.

Her heart shot into overdrive and when it resumed to its normal pace she found herself somehow less delighted with how the tree-cutting expedition had turned out.

If tree cutting was all about making memories, then what sort of memories would she tuck away for today? Ones that would keep her awake at night?

Zach was leaving in a little over two weeks. Where was her spin on that fact? They were friends again. That was good. They laughed and shared companionably, like old times.

Emma bit her lip as despair threatened. Her

own self-talk failed to cheer her up. There was no way to spin the fact that she really didn't want Zach Norman to leave and she didn't know how she was going to stop him.

Chapter Ten

"I am not sick." Emma coughed again, startling herself.

Good grief, she sounded like a barking seal, which hardly helped her defense strategy. She glanced at the plastic storage bins filled with her treasured Christmas ornaments that sat unopened around the beautiful and undecorated Virginia pine she and Zach had brought home last Wednesday, and moaned.

"Even if I was sick," she continued. "I don't have time to be sick. There's decorating to do and cookies to bake."

"Is that right?" Travis said. "You have a fever, your face is red and you just lost your lunch, but you aren't sick."

"Circumstantial evidence. I'm fine."

"No, you aren't." He took off his Stetson and ran a hand through his hair. "I always figured I was the stubborn one, but little sister, you've got me beat hands down."

"What are you doing here anyhow, Travis? Who's running the ranch?"

"Zach sent me over when you didn't show up for church this morning or tree sales at noon, and Dutch is running the ranch."

"That Zach Norman is such a troublemaker." Emma huffed and offered him a frustrated frown. "And if Dutch Stevens is running the ranch, then we all should drop to our knees and start praying."

"How about if I take you to urgent care?" Travis asked.

"What? No." She paused. "I mean, no thank you. I'm fine."

"Fine?"

"Yes. I ate something that didn't agree with me last night so I stayed home from church. Today, I fell asleep after I put the girls down for a nap and forgot to set the alarm."

He stared at her for a moment and then laughed. "That's a cow patty story if ever I heard one."

She crossed her arms and tried not to pout like her twins. "It is not."

"Emma, everyone gets sick. Even you. You've been going nonstop, skipping meals and sleep, and not taking care of yourself."

"Who told you that?"

Travis didn't answer.

"Zach Norman has a big mouth, too," Emma said. "I'll be at the tree tent in a bit. Let me get cleaned up. I couldn't possibly stay home this afternoon. We're already down two people."

"We have a ranch with sixty kids. If you step one foot on Big Heart, you'll infect half of them and the staff."

There was no argument for that logic, so she picked up a couch pillow from the floor and put it back in its proper location. Emma glanced around. The place was a disaster. Apparently, the girls had brought most of their toys into the living room while she was napping.

Napping in the middle of the day. What kind of mother was she? Emma eyed the trail of cereal on the floor leading to the hallway. Her fault for leaving the Crunchy-O's in plain sight. It was a very good thing every single drawer and cupboard was so locked down with childproof gadgets that even Houdini would be hard-pressed to figure it out.

"Are you listening?" Travis asked.

"I am, though you seem to be repeating yourself."

"Em, you have the flu."

"I had my flu shot."

"Doesn't matter."

"Fine. You had me at infecting the kids. I'll stay home."

He paced back and forth across the living room. "Lucy obviously can't come over. Or Jack."

"What are you talking about? Nobody needs to come over."

He kept rambling as though she wasn't there. "Normally, AJ would be here in a heartbeat to help you with the kids, but there's a possibility she could be…you know."

Emma perked up. "Are you saying I'm going to be an aunt, again?"

He grinned. "Looks like. Isn't that something? We're not announcing it yet, so let's keep that our secret until she checks in with her doctor."

"Yes. Absolutely." She coughed and quickly covered her mouth. "Germs! Stand back!"

Travis moved to the door.

"Well, now I know why you're all twisted up," Emma said. "You're going to be a daddy."

"Nice try. We're talking about you."

"You won. I agreed to stay home today. End of subject."

"I checked with your usual sitter, Sarah, but she's not available until tonight. But don't worry, I will find someone to help you with the girls."

"The girls are fine, I don't need help. Frankly, it's Zach I'm worried about."

"Zach? Why?"

"He's now in charge of my team and Lucy's."

"Your team's work is essentially complete. Dutch is helping with the tree sales and our college student wranglers are all putting in extra hours while they're on Christmas break."

"Wonderful." She frowned. "What if you run out of gingerbread?"

"You froze enough for six armies, Emma."

"That might possibly be true."

He reached for the doorknob. "I'll have someone check on you later."

"I don't need checking on. I'm a mom. Moms don't get sick."

Travis snorted. "That's what all moms say right before they get sick."

When the door closed behind her brother, Emma tiptoed to the girls' bedroom. They were sitting on the floor, completely absorbed in a movie with an animated bright blue tang fish. Since they had watched this movie no less than fifty times, Emma knew that the little fish would be done providing a life lesson in approximately fourteen and a half minutes. Enough time for a fast shower.

She darted into the shower and then donned clean jeans and a green sweatshirt with a red reindeer decorating the front. Rubbing at the condensation on the mirror, she frowned at her reflection. Her face was pale and her eyes dull. Even the holiday shirt failed to brighten her pallor. "I refuse to let any flu get the best of me," she said aloud.

Emma set out wooden puzzles for the girls

and then put snack crackers and juice boxes on the coffee table. Exhausted from the effort, she flopped on the couch, distressed by the fact that she actually felt worse. She didn't even have the energy to comb out her wet hair.

This wasn't good. Despite her declaration to the contrary, the flu bug had the upper hand and she was running out of options.

When the doorbell rang, she dragged herself across the room and yanked the door open. "Travis, I told you…"

Emma looked up to see Zach on her doorstep with two grocery sacks. "Oh, it's you."

He nodded. "That's right. It's me or Dutch. Take your pick."

"I don't need—"

He raised a palm and glowered at her. "I'm not going to argue with you. Me or Dutch?"

"Hmm. John Wayne or Oscar the Grouch. This is a tough decision."

"Hurry up before we both freeze."

"Fine. Come in. Make yourself at home. Nice of you to drop by unannounced."

He stomped the snow off his boots and strode into the house. "Great tree."

"It's not even decorated," she said and began to cough.

"You sound awful. A cough like that could knock a person into next week, Emma. You need to rest."

"Thank you, I'll take that under advisement."

"Do you feel like you look?"

"Don't sugarcoat it, Zach." Annoyed with the current situation, Emma grabbed a box of tissues, cradled them to her chest and resumed her exile on the couch. "If I have the flu, then why am I coughing?"

Zach kicked the door shut and walked into the kitchen. He placed the grocery sacks on the kitchen island. "I didn't bring medical advice, only groceries. I have no idea." He glanced around. "So this is where the amazing chocolate muffins are made, huh?"

"Yes. Feel free to inspect. Tours start in an hour."

"You're very amusing for a sick woman."

She blew her nose. "Unauthorized illness brings out the best in me."

Zach began to pull cans and jars from the paper bags.

"What do you have there?" she asked.

"I have no idea. Lucy ordered me to bring these." He held up a package. "Microwave mashed potatoes. Looks like comfort food to me. Where should I put this?"

"Lower left cupboard."

Zach tugged on the handle. "It's locked." He tried another cupboard. "They all seem to be locked." He stared at her. "Why are the cupboards locked?"

"Childproofing. A strategic part of good parenting. You lock them out of everything and then send them out into the world eighteen years later." She waved a hand in the air. "The keys are on top of the fridge."

"Unca Zach?" Rachel peeked into the living room from the hallway, a questioning expression on her face. She tiptoed farther into the room. "Unca Zach! Bit. Come. Come. Unca Zach is here."

A moment later Elizabeth showed up, with a bedraggled stuffed animal in tow. She was less enthusiastic, yet willing to offer her uncle a smile and a good word. "Unca Zach!"

"'Bit'?" he asked Emma as he swooped down and picked up Rachel in one arm and Elizabeth in the other.

"It's the newest language twist around here. Rachel finds it easier than Elizabeth," Emma said.

"Mommy sick," Rachel said. "Pway."

"We're going to take good care of Mommy," Zach said.

"Pway," Rachel repeated.

Emma smiled at her daughter. "They want you to—"

"Yeah, I got that part. I'm stalling."

"You know how it works. They won't give up until you do."

Zach sighed and bowed his head. "Dear Lord,

please help Rachel and Bit's mommy feel better. Amen."

The girls nodded with approval.

He met Emma's gaze and gave a sympathetic smile. "I'm sorry you're sick."

"I'm not..."

Zach's expression stopped her.

She could only sigh. There was no point denying it anymore. Her resistance had slipped the moment he stepped into the room. Now that he stood in the middle of her house like a knight in flannel armor, holding her children and even praying, she gave up all pretense. Her heart began to melt around the edges and her eyes teared up in response. Everything was going to be all right now that Zach was here.

Clutching the tissue box tightly, Emma stood. "I'm sick."

"Yes, you are," Zach agreed. He peered closer. "Em, are you crying?"

"No! I have the flu! My eyes are watering. Look it up on WebMD."

"Sheesh, relax. I believe you."

"I'm going to sleep until I feel better. They're all yours."

"Wise decision, Emma."

Wise, maybe, but she hated not being in control.

Sleep came quickly and when she woke, sunlight was streaming into the room, temporarily blinding and disorienting her. Emma held a hand to her eyes and stumbled into the hallway. "Rachel? Elizabeth? What time is it?"

"It's okay, Miss Emma. They're taking a nap."

"Sarah?" Emma blinked and looked around while straightening her rumpled jeans and a wrinkled sweatshirt. "How long have you been here?" She stared dumbfounded at the babysitter at the kitchen table reading a book. "How long have I been here?"

"I spent the night."

"The night? What? Don't you have classes?"

"Christmas break."

"Wait. Back up. What day is this?"

"Monday."

"Monday?" Emma rubbed her eyes. "I've been out for like twenty hours."

"Mr. Norman said to let you sleep."

"Bless you for that, Sarah. Now I need to talk to Zach. I have a meeting at Randall Ranch that I most likely missed and a video conference in the afternoon."

Sarah stood and came into the living room. She put a gentle hand on Emma's shoulder. "Miss Emma, it's okay. Mr. Norman said to tell you he would meet with the rancher and he planned to handle the RangePro stuff today. You're supposed to concentrate on getting better."

"I'll try, but I have to warn you. I'm a terrible patient."

"Yes. Mr. Norman said that, too."

Emma frowned. Of course he did. She looked around the room, confused. Gone were the mashed bits of cereal from the carpet. The blocks and toys had disappeared, as well. "Why is it so tidy in here?"

"Your house is always tidy."

"Oh, it wasn't yesterday."

Sarah cocked her head and glanced at the living room. "This is how I found it when I came over last evening."

Emma caught a flash of light from the corner of her eye. She turned to look at the Christmas tree and gasped.

The beautiful Virginia pine stood regally in the corner with an angel crown on the top. Tiny holiday lights decorated the branches. They'd been strung from inside the branches to the outside, exactly the way she preferred. The lights were plugged in and now twinkled holiday cheer. A glittery tinsel garland had been evenly wrapped around the branches of the tree, as well. Why, even the ornaments were hung correctly, positioned to hide the bare spots between the branches. "The tree. It's decorated." She sighed. "It's so Christmassy."

Sarah nodded. "Yes. Mr. Norman and the girls were doing that when I arrived last evening." She pulled her phone from her pocket. "I took a few pictures for you."

"Oh, my!" Emotion slammed into Emma at the sight of the navy SEAL helping the toddlers put ornaments on the tree. "I don't even have words. Can you send them to my cell?"

"Absolutely."

"Thank you, Sarah." Emma shook her head. "So basically it looks like Zach Norman is perfect. Would that be about right?"

Sarah giggled. "Yes, and he's very handsome, too, isn't he?"

Emma grinned. "Yes. I'm with you on that." She tried to run a hand through her hair, but the tangles swallowed her fingers. "Ugh."

"There's chicken soup in the fridge," Sarah said. "Homemade."

"If you try to tell me that Zach made homemade chicken soup, I'm going to know this is a hallucination."

"No, AJ, I mean, Mrs. Maxwell brought it over. It has chicken and egg noodles. Really yummy. The girls had some for lunch."

"You know what? I'm going to give Mr. Norman a call. If I can verify this is not a hallucination, I'll be back for soup."

Sarah laughed. "Okay. I'll start warming up the pot."

Emma started down the hall then stopped and turned back. "Thank you again, Sarah."

"You're very welcome." She hesitated. "Mr. Norman is very, um, fond of you."

"Zach? Do you think so?"

Sarah gave a shy nod.

"It's my chocolate muffins. They bring grown men to their knees."

"I don't think that's it."

"Rachel and Elizabeth. He loves the twins."

"Miss Emma, he loves the twins, but he was fretting about you."

Zach? Fretting? It was going to take a minute or two to digest that information.

Emma hurried down the hall and did a double take when she saw herself in the hall mirror. Her hair had dried wet and was now bent, and folded and stuck out at odd angles. She looked like the nightmare before Christmas.

Grabbing a hairbrush and a clip from a bureau, Emma grabbed her cell phone. She checked the time. Uh-oh. By now, Zach had no doubt already met with Beau Randall.

Zach, who'd taken an instant dislike to the rich rancher, had gone to the meeting for her. That was taking one for the team.

She had really wanted to introduce Zach to RangePro slowly. Instead, she'd put him on a bull and sent him into the arena. Poor Zach. If the man wasn't planning his exit strategy already, he soon would be. And it was her fault.

Zach pulled into the admin parking lot of Big Heart Ranch. He cut the engine and cracked the window, hoping the blast of frigid air would douse his fiery anger before he called to check on Emma.

Beau Randall was all hat and no cattle. The man had zero barn cred. Randall wasn't a rancher, and he didn't know a thing about ranching. He had never even seen a heifer up close and had no plans to. Since day one, the beautiful Pawhuska ranch had been outsourced to a team of high-paid wranglers.

The rich investor sat on horses that someone else tacked up while he concentrated on his next moneymaking scheme.

Today Randall decided that his next venture was taking over RangePro. Six weeks ago, Zach would have been overjoyed at the prospect. Now he understood what the company meant to Emma. Randall didn't have a clue, nor would he care that his plan would break her heart.

The whole situation didn't bode well for him, either. Emma would conclude he and Randall were in cahoots. Sure, she would. And why not?

She sends a guy who doesn't like her husband's company into a meeting with a rattlesnake and he comes out without signing the deal and with a cash buyout offer on the table from said snake.

It sounded shady to him, too, and he'd been there. There had to be a workable solution. He'd told Emma there was weeks ago, but now he was under the gun to fix this mess before Emma found out.

His phone rang, and he grimaced when the screen display showed it was Emma. If he didn't answer, she'd turn up at Big Heart before he could put the parking brake on.

Zach hit Accept Call. "Emma, why aren't you resting?"

"I've been sleeping since yesterday."

"That's a start."

"A start?" she sputtered. "I've got crease marks on my face. If I sleep any more, they'll be permanent."

Zach laughed. "You might be exaggerating."

"Not much." She paused. "How's everything going with RangePro?"

There was an underlying excitement in Emma's voice. She was expecting big things from today's meeting and he wasn't going to be the one to let her down when she was so vulnerable.

"Was this all a plot to get me to handle RangePro?" Zach asked. "You think I'm a half-baked cowboy with a bum knee, so you're trying to get me behind a desk like everyone else, right?"

"A diabolical plot it is, if I staged my own illness," Emma returned. "For the record, you could never be a half-baked anything, Zach Norman, and I won't let you disparage yourself."

"Hmm. You sound better," he noted.

"I feel better, thank you. And thanks for decorating the tree and everything else you did."

"My pleasure."

"Pretty good work for a Scrooge."

"I'll take that as a compliment."

"So, um, you had your appointment with Randall. How did it go? Were you able to lock him in?"

"Not exactly. Mr. Randall was disappointed that you were unable to be there and very annoyed when he found out that I'm the other half of RangePro."

"That doesn't sound good."

"He didn't sign, Emma."

There was a moment of silence.

"Emma? You still there?"

"Yes."

"I'm really sorry."

"Well, you tried, right? And you didn't call him out for being a city slicker or insult him for being from Texas, did you?"

"I was on my best behavior."

"So he didn't sign. That makes me as disappointed as Beau Randall. I had hoped that if he did, we might get more clients from his tax bracket and maybe the company could expand. Steve would have liked that."

Silence stretched before she finally said, "Did he mention why?"

"He has some other ideas he's pursuing."

"Really?" Her voice perked up. "Anything I might be interested in?"

"You and I can sit down and have a long talk about Randall once you're well and back in the office."

"Okay, but what about the video conference with my reps and tech? You need my computer passwords. Hang on, let me open my laptop."

"Whoa. Whoa. Emma, I canceled. It can wait."

There was a long pause.

"You're frowning, aren't you?"

"Possibly."

"Did you try the soup?"

"Everyone is pushing soup," she muttered. "I'll try the soup when I'm done wallowing in self-pity."

"I'm sorry, Emma."

"What? No. It's not your fault. I knew all along that Randall was a long shot."

Zach put a hand on the steering wheel. "Was there anything else?" he asked.

"No. I suppose not. I have a field appointment tomorrow. A little mom-and-pop sheep ranch outside of town. I need to be back in the office soon."

"I'll ask Iris to reschedule," Zach said.

"No. I feel so much better. I'm sure this was simply a twenty-four-hour bug."

"Let's compromise. I'll help you with anything you want that has to do with RangePro this week if you stay home until Wednesday."

"One more day?" she returned.

"Yes."

She groaned.

"Did I mention that this is a onetime offer that expires—" he checked his watch "—in five minutes?"

"I'll take it, though I don't understand why you'd offer. You hate RangePro."

"I don't hate my brother's company. I'm proud of him for what he accomplished. But RangePro isn't my future."

"Because it was Steve's company, or because you have other plans?"

"Both. RangePro is Steve's business and Steve's dream." He paused. "Emma, I'm not Steve. Are you okay with that?"

"I don't want you to be Steve. I like you just the way you are," she said softly.

"Thank you," he said.

"Zach?"

"Yeah?"

"I mean it. I'm not trying to make you into Steve. I'm sorry if it seemed that way."

"Nothing to be sorry about. Now we have a deal and you're going to go eat soup and rest."

"How's the Holiday Roundup going?"

"Terrific. According to your sister, tree sales have doubled. She ordered another half truckload and it will be delivered today."

"She's working from home, right?"

"Absolutely."

"And everything else?"

"Dutch is playing Santa Claus for the kids at the Pawhuska Orphanage tonight."

"Oh, I'm going to miss that."

"I'll have someone take pictures for you."

"What else is going on?" she asked.

"The entire cast and crew of the live nativity are playing to a full house every night. They only lost the sheep twice."

"They lost the sheep?"

"An oversight."

"Twice?" Emma laughed. "I'm afraid to ask what else."

"The bell ringers and carolers have not frozen and the *Timber Independence* gave your gingerbread a three-star rating."

"Really?"

"I might be exaggerating. I learned from the best."

Emma laughed. "I'm missing Christmas out there in the world."

"It will still be here on Wednesday."

Her only response was a dramatic sigh.

"I'll stop by on Tuesday night," Zach said.

"You will?" It was a small, hopeful plea.

"Yes, and I'll bring dinner, too."

"That would be wonderful, Zach."

"Now go rest. And give the girls a kiss for me."

"Yes. I'll do that, and thank you, Zach. For all your help."

"You're welcome."

Zach set down the phone and rubbed a hand over his face. He hated that he hadn't given her the full story on Randall. The omission burned his gut and tore at his heart.

But how was he going to tell Emma that not only was Beau Randall not interested in becoming her number one client, but the man wanted to buy her out and shut down RangePro to launch his own livestock management software enterprise?

He knew Emma and he knew that she was convinced she could have turned Randall around if she had been the one at the meeting instead of him. This time her considerable charm would not be enough to finesse the situation.

The entire thing was a no-win disaster waiting to happen. If she found out, she'd be upset he didn't tell her, and if he told her she'd shoot the messenger.

Right about now he'd like to shoot Beau Randall.

Zach had an ominous feeling that hovered like dark clouds before a storm. It was a sick feeling that things were about to get a whole lot worse before they got better.

Chapter Eleven

"When she opens the door, you can start," Zach said to the group assembling on Emma's porch. He tucked a hand into his pocket to be sure the package was still there. Maybe he'd get a chance to give Emma her Christmas present tonight.

Her words from weeks ago came back to him. *Christmas isn't about receiving, it's about giving.*

Tonight was all about giving back to Emma.

He smiled to himself. From putting up Holiday Roundup lights to working with Mick and Benjie to spending time with Emma and his nieces, the list of what he'd received since he arrived went on and on. Emma had given him back the hope that he still had something to contribute.

Around him, ranch staff in period costume looked like they'd stepped straight out of a stage production of a Charles Dickens Christmas play as they lined up. Of course, as everyone reminded him, Emma had been responsible for the authentic reproduction Victorian dresses and shawls, capes and hats.

Snow remained on the ground, though the walkway to Emma's front porch was clear. The December air was crisp and the sky above provided a vivid and endless canvas of coral as the sun began to set. The troupe of performers stood next to a tall conifer, adding to the backdrop for the evening's live performance.

Tonight the Big Heart Ranch players offered cheerful nods and grins as they stood ready to serenade Emma with "fa-la-la-la-la" and bell ringing.

"Are you sure she's not still sick?" someone asked.

"She texted me fifteen times today with instructions and reminders," Zach said. "Our Emma is on the mend and planning to be in the office tomorrow morning."

After hours of tossing and turning Monday night, unable to figure out a way to thwart Beau Randall, Zach had finally gotten up, only to discover endless versions of *A Christmas Carol* playing on the local television channel. Apparently, the movies played repeatedly throughout the season. He practically had the dialogue memorized after the third film.

That was when the idea to bring Christmas to Emma hit him. He prayed it was as good an idea tonight as it seemed at 3:00 a.m.

Zach rang the doorbell and stepped to the side of the porch and out of the direct line of sight.

The front light came on, illuminating the group, and then the door slowly opened, setting the wreath into a slow sway.

"What's this?" Emma said. She stood in the doorway in her ugly Christmas sweater, staring with disbelief as the singers burst into a hearty rendition of "We Wish You a Merry Christmas." Her face lit up as they continued. A moment later Rachel and Elizabeth peeked out from behind their mother's denim-clad legs, eyes round as they, too, watched, mesmerized.

Not to be outdone, the Big Heart Ranch bell ringers edged to the front ready to begin as the singers concluded with the final refrain of "...and a happy New Year."

"Wait!" Emma called. "It's freezing. Please, come in the house and we'll continue where it's warm."

Laughter and good-natured chatter filled the air as they filed into the little house. Zach stood in place, not sure what to do.

"Zach? Are you coming?" Emma called. She stepped around the porch pillar and met his gaze with a tender smile.

"Uh, yeah. How'd you know I was here?"

"Oh, Zach, I always know when you're around."

Words escaped him when she took his large

hand in hers and tugged him inside. At that moment, he would have followed her anywhere. His heart wasn't on his sleeve—it was right there in her hand.

An hour later, the singers and bell ringers departed, though not until Emma handed out artfully decorated cutout cookies.

Zach held Rachel and Elizabeth as Emma waved goodbye to her guests from the front door. There was a sense of rightness as the four of them filled the doorway of the house.

"Cowd, Momma." Rachel shivered and tucked herself closer to Zach.

"Oh, sorry, sweetie." Emma shut the front door and put the platter of cookies on the coffee table before smiling up at Zach. "That was the nicest thing. I can't believe you did that."

"You said you were missing out on Christmas."

"I know, but I didn't expect… Come on, that was perfect. I couldn't have planned a better surprise myself."

"That's quite a compliment coming from the queen of Christmas."

"And you deserve the accolades."

"How did you have Christmas cookies ready to give them?" he asked.

"I baked today."

"Of course, you did."

She stood straight. "I'm feeling much better and it's not Christmas without my cutout cookies."

"Didn't you make them for the Christmas party?"

"Oh, that was…" She stopped. "Oh, my. That was early November. Over six weeks ago. It doesn't count."

But Zach had been counting. Six and a half weeks. Eleven days before he headed back to California to get his stuff from storage and move on to his new job. Every day the calendar mocked him as though it was well aware that he didn't want to go anywhere.

The doorbell rang and Emma's eyes rounded. "What now?"

His gaze went to the wall clock. "Pizza. Right on time. I don't know about you, but I'm starving." He eased the twins down and opened the door.

"I've got cash right here," Emma called.

"No way. I planned this dinner with my favorite girls. Besides, the pizza was paid for when I placed the order," Zach said. He handed the teenage delivery driver a tip and grabbed the boxes.

"Wow," the youth said, with a glance at the crumpled bill in his hand. "Thanks a lot, mister. Merry Christmas."

"Yeah. You, too."

Sliding the boxes onto the counter, he met Emma's questioning expression. "What?" he asked, trying to hide a smile.

"You seem to have had a holiday epiphany, not unlike old Ebenezer."

"Nope. I'm just happy." He winked at her.

"Oh. Well, that's good, too." Flustered, she looked away and opened a pizza box.

Stomach grumbling, he inhaled the rich scent of sauce and spices. "I went with a cheese pizza for the girls and an everything pizza for us. Anchovies are only on your half."

Emma laughed, her eyes widening with surprise. "You remembered." She pulled dishes from the cupboard.

"Hard to forget that you dared me to eat a salty little forage fish."

"You said you liked them."

"Yeah. That wasn't exactly the truth. You challenged me."

"See, even back then you were destined to be a hero. Courage in the face of adversity."

"Hero nothing. I was trying to impress you."

"Really?" She turned from the silverware drawer. "You were trying to impress me?"

"Wasn't it obvious?"

"No."

"Emma, I spent most of my youth trying to get your attention."

"I never knew." The words were a soft admission as her dark eyes met his.

He held his breath, not sure what to say.

"Want pizza!" Rachel cried.

Zach blinked, relieved at the interruption. His emotions were moving way ahead of his brain tonight.

"Time to wash your hands, little ladies," Emma said.

Emma sat safely across from him, holding the girls' hands, as he did from the other side of the small oak table, when they bowed their heads for grace. Whispering "amen," he raised his head and slowly looked around. Someday, Rachel and Elizabeth would understand how fortunate they were to have a mother who loved them and put faith and family first.

The twins giggled with excitement as Emma cut their pizza into bite-size pieces. He slid two slices of pizza onto a plate and found himself staring at the scene in front of him, committing the memory to a special place in his heart.

"Everything okay, Zach?" Emma asked.

"Everything is perfect, Em."

"Want an anchovy?" She dangled a slimy piece toward him.

"I'll pass." He shuddered when she bit into her slice of pizza.

"Seriously? The big navy SEAL is afraid of an anchovy?"

"Yeah, it's my kryptonite," he said. *Like you and the girls*, he silently amended.

"Good pizza," Rachel said.

"Tell Uncle Zach thank you, girls."

Both Rachel and Elizabeth echoed, "Thank you, Unca Zach."

"You're welcome, Rachel and Bit." He picked up a napkin and wiped a spot of sauce from Rachel's nose before digging in to his own meal.

"You're quiet tonight," Emma said as she finished her pizza. "What are you thinking about?"

"I'm thinking that you're a wonderful mother."

"Thank you, but look at yourself, handling toddlers like a pro. You've turned out to be a pretty great uncle."

"No one is more surprised than me," he said. "I should have stepped up to the role sooner." The realization ached. He had missed too much by being stubborn.

"You've had a lot going on with recuperating. Dutch says you had three surgeries."

"Dutch again." Zach shook his head and chuckled. "Telling Dutch something is like writing it on a chalkboard in the stables."

Emma offered a rueful smile of acknowledgment. "It's true, right? Your knee is why you left the navy."

"Yeah. They wanted to put me behind a desk, too."

"Well, we're glad you're here. It would be nice to have you around all the time."

Zach jerked his head up at the words. "I... Really?"

"Yes," she said softly.

A soft thump had him turning his head. "Look," he said with a nod toward Elizabeth. The toddler's eyes kept closing, and her head bobbed with the effort of staying awake.

"It's way past their bedtime." Emma slid her chair back. "I'm going to get them ready for bed."

Zach stood and kissed the twins on their silky heads. "Good night, ladies."

"You aren't leaving yet, are you?" Emma asked.

"Not until I finish KP."

"Kitchen duty is not necessary."

"It's only a few dishes. I'll be done before you are."

Clearing the table, he washed the dishes, wrapped the pizza in foil and slid it into the fridge.

Zach stood outside the girls' room and whispered past the partially open door. "Emma, where are your trash cans?"

The door opened and Emma hurried out, nearly running into him.

"Whoa." Zach held her by the shoulders. "Careful."

Emma shot him a stern expression. "Oh, no

you don't. You've already done too much already. Leave the trash."

He laughed and removed his hands. "Easy there, Mom. It's only trash."

"Leave it. I have something to show you."

Zach followed her to the living room, where the Christmas tree glowed in the corner, warming the room with its soft holiday lights. She pulled a box from the bookshelf and handed it to him.

"What's this?"

"Christmas in a box."

"Oh, yeah?" He lifted the lid. "DVDs?"

"I hand selected some of my very favorite holiday movies for you."

"Thank you."

"Now, promise me you'll try to watch at least a couple."

Zach flipped through the stack. "For sure the Snoopy one."

"Snoopy? What about Bing Crosby?"

"I'll see what I can do." He looked at her and cleared his throat, surprised to discover he now had the perfect segue to give Emma her gift. So why was he suddenly nervous? "I have something for you, too."

"You do?"

"Yeah. I know it's not Christmas yet."

"It will be. In four days and six hours," Emma said.

"You have that memorized?"

"I do."

He grabbed his coat from the kitchen chair and dug in the pocket. "This is for you."

Her gaze went from the silver box with the fancy silver bow up to him before she hesitantly took the package from his hands. "I, ah…"

"Open it now."

"It isn't Christmas."

"I know. Four days and six hours. But I promise you, this will make Christmas even better."

Emma put a hand to her heart. "Who are you and what have you done with Scrooge?"

"He's changing. I'll give you that."

"Yes, he is." She examined the package. "Did you wrap this?"

He blew a raspberry. "Not hardly. Why?"

"I like to open my packages with abandon, but if you wrapped it with care, all by yourself, I'll show some restraint."

"Go for it."

Grinning, she tore the bow off, pulling the black box from the paper before opening the flip lid.

Emma's soft gasp was followed by a heartfelt sigh. "A Christmas watch. The one from the store window."

He nodded. The gaudy watch with a red band and a faux-jeweled Christmas tree rested on the box's satin lining. Tiny bits of colored glass dotted the tree, and a golden jewel rested on top.

"It's beautiful." She removed the clock piece from the satin lining, fumbling when she attempted to put it on herself.

"Let me help."

Zach was no better. His hands trembled as he circled the watchband around Emma's slim wrist and fastened the clasp. "Too tight?" he asked.

Her gaze met his. "It's perfect."

His lips twitched. "Matches your ugly Christmas sweater, too."

"So it does," Emma murmured.

"There's a button on the side. It plays 'Rocking Around the Christmas Tree.' Let me show you."

The soft musical notes filled the silent room. Zach looked down and realized her hand was still in his.

"Thank you, Zach. This is the best Christmas present ever."

"I'm not sure that's true, but trust me, it comes from the heart." He smiled. "Merry Christmas, Emma."

He leaned down to kiss her cheek, but Emma shifted her head slightly. Her lips met his in a soft collision. It was a small kiss, yet powerful enough to ignite the tiny spark of hope that had been waiting patiently deep inside him all these years.

When she sighed and leaned against him, Zach allowed himself to hold her as though she was his, knowing only too well the risk he was taking.

Could he stay at Big Heart Ranch? Was a future with Emma and the girls really within his grasp? Or was he fooling himself again?

Emma's head popped up when the front door of the admin building opened. The last three days she'd kept her door open whenever possible, hoping to hear the familiar sound of boots hitting the floor outside her office.

Yes, that was definitely the sound of boots.

A male voice greeted the receptionist and Emma's heart turned over.

It was Zach. She hadn't seen him since Tuesday night, well, except in her daydreams when she relived the lovely kiss they'd shared. Fingering her bangs into place, Emma reached for her lip gloss and straightened her red sweater.

Two kisses in all. Did they mean anything to Zach?

Or did they mean much too much to her?

He gave a rap on the door frame and stuck his head in, offering a broad grin. "Ho. Ho. Ho."

Emma melted at the sight. Zach had transformed since he arrived at the ranch. The tightness around his mouth indicating pain had diminished, as had his limp. Now he smiled often and the cheerful expression he wore looked good on him.

"Come on in, Zach."

He pulled the box of DVDs from behind him and placed it on her desk.

"You watched them all. Already?"

"Yeah. Not a big deal. I've had a touch of insomnia."

"It is a big deal, though I'm sorry you can't sleep."

"Aren't you going to ask me which was my favorite?"

"Sounds like you want to tell me."

"A Christmas Carol."

"That wasn't in the box."

"Yeah, and to tell you the truth, I was a little disappointed that you failed to include Dickens. It's a classic. Maybe we can discuss the symbolism in the story sometime."

"Sure. We can do that." Emma faltered. "Symbolism?"

"Uh-huh. So, besides the good cheer about reforming Ebenezer Scrooge, how are you feeling?" he asked.

"Wonderful. I signed up to move cattle on Monday."

"Emma, you've been riding shotgun on the entire Holiday Roundup. Monday is the day after Christmas. Let someone else move the herd. You deserve a break."

"First of all, you're the one who made the roundup a success. You stepped in on every issue that came up. I feel like a slacker."

He crossed his arms and offered his usual dismissal of his contribution.

"Second, I just came off of a three-day break, Zach. I can handle cattle. Besides, we're running out of wranglers."

"I'll do it then," Zach said. "And you can believe that my good buddy Dutch is going to assist." He sat down in the chair on the other side of her desk. "Can't believe tomorrow is Christmas Eve."

"Yes, and I have all of my family here this year."

"My first Christmas on Big Heart Ranch." He fiddled with the miniature snowman on her desk. "I'm looking forward to watching Rachel and Elizabeth open presents."

"They made you a special gift. You wouldn't believe how excited they are to give it to you."

"I can't wait. You know, it means a lot that you're welcoming me into your holiday. I'm accustomed to doors closing this time of year. Most folks don't want a stranger in the middle of their celebrations." He bowed his head then met her gaze. "You were right all along. It's not hype around here. The holiday spirit is real at Big Heart Ranch."

"Oh, Zach. It means the world to me to hear you say that."

"It's the truth." He reached across the desk and caught her fingers.

Emma looked up and warmed at the tenderness in his gray eyes.

"Nice watch," he murmured. "Very classy."

She grinned. "I love this watch. I've been annoying everyone by playing the little song all day."

"Good for you!" A smile pulled at his lips as he released her hand and relaxed in the chair.

"Have you talked to your dad? Or your mother?" Emma asked.

"Sent my father and stepmother a quick text. They're somewhere off the Amalfi Coast. As for my mother, the day I left for college was the last day I saw her."

"Is there a possibility you could reach out to her? It's been a long time."

"Emma," he warned. "I'm sitting in the chair, but this isn't a session."

"I'm speaking as your friend. It seems perfectly obvious that you can't go forward while your past is chasing you down. Big Heart Ranch is all about that. This is the place where we let go of our past. New beginnings. Like the birth of our Lord at Christmas."

"You're having a Christmas overdose again."

"Not at all. All I'm saying is that forgiveness frees you."

"Emma, with all due respect, what do you know about forgiveness?"

She inhaled sharply at his words. "I know plenty. Trust and forgiveness go hand in hand. I've lost everything I had twice in my life, and yet, given that, I'm willing to trust again. Willing to forgive, because I know your way doesn't bring happiness."

Zach rubbed the base of his hand on his forehead.

"What's the worst that can happen, Zach?"

"You're right, I'm handicapped in more ways than my knee. I'll give your words some serious thought and prayer."

"Thank you." She leaned back in her chair, delighted at his response. "That's all I ask."

When Emma's desk phone rang, Zach stood. "I won't keep you."

She waved for him to sit down and reached for the receiver. "It's Beau Randall," she said. "Hang on."

Zach slowly settled back into the chair, discomfort in his expression.

"Hi there, Beau. Merry Christmas. Do you mind if I put you on speaker? Zach is in the office with me."

Emma pressed the button and returned the receiver to the cradle.

"What can I do for you, Beau?"

"As I explained to Mr. Norman, I'm ready to make a deal."

She straightened in her chair and shot Zach an excited glance. "That's wonderful. Did Zach explain our ninety-day money-back guarantee?

And I hope he gave you the information regarding the amazing service agreement we provide."

"No. Not that kind of deal. I'm talking about a cash buyout. I want to purchase RangePro."

"What?" Emma's smile faded and her stomach clenched. She glanced out her office window. The sun had gone into hiding behind the clouds.

"Didn't he tell you?"

She looked to Zach, but he wouldn't meet her eyes. "No, but it's been so busy here with our Holiday Roundup, and me out of the office earlier in the week. I'm sure it slipped Mr. Norman's mind."

Beau laughed. "Hard to let the numbers I offered slip anything, if you ask me. I'm guessing you're a shrewd negotiator, Emma."

"Oh, you have no idea," she murmured. "Do you mind if I ask why the sudden interest in RangePro?"

"I'm launching my own web-based livestock management program. RangePro will be absorbed into that."

"You mean it will go away." Emma picked up a pen and gripped it like a lifeline.

"Semantics."

"Do you mind if I get back to you?"

"Sure, but as I said, if you're holding out for a better price, I'm willing to discuss the options. Just don't sell to someone else before you talk to me." He paused. "I like you, Emma, but the offer only stands until the end of the year. Then you're on your own."

"What makes you think I'm interested in selling?"

"You'd be a fool not to."

"Have a wonderful Christmas, Beau." She depressed the end call button and swallowed hard. "Why didn't you tell me?" The words were a flat refrain, bouncing off the walls of her office.

"What was the point? You don't want to sell."

"You're still pressing for a sale. An end to RangePro."

"Are you asking me or telling me?"

"Oh, I'm definitely asking."

This time he did look at her, and his eyes were hard. "I don't care if you sell the company or keep it. My life is unchanged either way."

The words sliced through her. She had her answer about how he felt. Two kisses meant nothing to Zach.

"Did you tell Beau that RangePro was for sale?" she asked.

Zach shook his head and released a long breath. "If you trusted me you would have never asked me that question."

"I do trust you."

He gave her his opinion of her words with a glance.

"Emma, Randall came up with the offer to buy RangePro all by himself. The moment I stepped onto his ranch, he made it clear that he did not intend to sign on the dotted line. He was after your company from day one, and he'll do whatever it takes to get it."

She looked at him, already regretting taking Beau Randall's call.

"Our company," she quietly corrected.

"I understand this is a shock, but think carefully about the facts. The man has a fortune at his disposal. He's offering you a chance to sell at a substantial profit before he pushes you out of the market. And he will. People like Beau Randall don't give up and they don't lose."

"I still don't understand why you didn't tell me."

"Because I'm a coward. I knew you'd jump to conclusions and believe I colluded with Randall."

"What was I supposed to think?"

"You tell me." He stood and his eyes became steely once again as he searched her face. Searched her soul. "Emma, I thought we were doing a slow dance toward the same promise. Looks like I was wrong. Again."

"I don't understand why Steve's company always seems to stand between us."

"Maybe it's Steve that's standing between us." Zach shook his head. "He's my brother and I'll always love him, but what you said not minutes ago is truer than I realized. Neither one of us can go forward while our past is chasing us down."

"You want me to let Steve go?"

"No, Emma. All I'm asking you to do is trust me enough to walk to your future." Bleakness filled the once smiling face as he turned to go.

"Will I see you tomorrow night at Lucy and Jack's for Christmas Eve?" Emma asked as panic began to claw at her.

"What would be the point?" He looked at her and shrugged. "I'm due in San Diego on the first to sign the paperwork on the new job before I ship out. I might as well get on the road."

Emma's heart clenched. *No. No. This can't be happening.*

Zach walked slowly down the hall, every echoing step a reminder of what she was losing, yet Emma's legs were leaden and she was unable to move. Unable to breach the distance between them.

"Merry Christmas, Mr. Norman," Iris called.

"Yeah, Merry Christmas," he returned.

The building door closed with a whoosh and a dull thud.

Christmas Eve without Zach. All her tomorrows without Zach.

Emma shivered. The room seemed colder as the startling reality hit. Zach had been in her heart her entire life, but somehow, somewhere, in the last eight weeks, everything had changed. What was she going to do?

Chapter Twelve

"Lucy, tell me what to do." Shavings of carrot peelings shot into the sink as Emma began to prep for the Christmas Eve vegetable lasagna. Her heart wasn't in the task.

"*Me?* I'm a terrible cook. Why do you think I invited you over?"

"I'm talking about Zach."

"I know even less about relationships than I do about cooking. If you recall, I held on to an empty house for years, too afraid to move on with my life." She shook her head as she slid the relish tray into the refrigerator. "And our dear brother is another example of cowardice in the face of cobwebs of the past. I'm afraid we Maxwells do not part with our baggage without a fight."

Emma released a pained groan.

"Too bad Rue Butterfield is out of town. Practical advice is her specialty. That and swift kicks. Sounds like you need both."

"Thanks a lot. Maybe I should talk to Dutch."

"I'd rely on Google before I believed anything Dutch offered. Well, except John Wayne trivia."

Emma wiped at her eyes with the corner of her prancing reindeer apron.

"Oh, honey, why are you crying?"

"I'm not crying. I'm cutting onions."

"Those are carrots," Lucy pointed out.

She whirled around with the vegetable clutched in her hand. "He's gone, Lucy. Gone. My daughters won't get to spend Christmas with Unca Zach and it's all my fault."

Lucy pulled out a kitchen chair. "Sit down. I'll make some nice hot tea and then we can figure this out."

"We don't have time to figure this out. The casserole isn't ready."

"You made twelve dozen Christmas cookies. We are not going to starve. Now sit." Her big sister pointed to a chair. "Don't make me pull rank on you!"

"Fine." Emma slid into the chair and put her forehead on the table.

"Aunt Emma, are you okay?" Dub Harris asked as he approached her.

"Yes, sweetie. My heart is just breaking," she mumbled into the red-and-green-plaid tablecloth.

"Emma!" Lucy hissed. "He's a kid."

Emma sat up straight. "I mean, I just need tea and I'll be fine."

The six-year-old circled her shoulders as best as he could with both arms, then rested his blond head on her right shoulder before squeezing tight.

"Aw, thanks so much, sweetie. Dub hugs are the best."

He offered a shy grin. "Do you want me to pray for you?"

Emma smiled. The kid was going to be a heart-breaker someday. Already he was melting hers with those big blue eyes. His lisp was gone now that his front teeth had emerged. Little Dub was growing up. Time was moving much too fast.

She patted his hand. "I'm much better now, but I'll keep that offer in mind if I need it later."

He nodded, pleased with the answer.

"Did you come in here for something, Dub?" Lucy asked as she set out mugs and herbal tea bags.

"My dad needs a rag. The puppy had an accident."

Lucy handed him a roll of paper towels and disinfectant spray. "Please ask your daddy to take the puppy to the basement. We have guests coming."

"Yes, ma'am."

"Thank you, Dubster."

"'My dad,' huh?" Emma smiled at the supreme cuteness she'd just witnessed.

"Isn't that adorable?" Lucy commented. "He's been saying that lately."

"Where did the puppy come from?"

"Early Christmas present. Dub has always wanted a puppy. How could I say no to a boy who has already had a chunk of his childhood stolen from him?"

"You have seven-year-old triplets and you are about to deliver." She stared at the red-and-green maternity top that barely covered her sister's abdomen. "A puppy is like bringing another baby into the house. What were you thinking?"

"Sometimes you don't think, you just feel."

Emma rolled her eyes. "Then there's the rest of us, who think and don't feel." She ran a finger over the face of her Christmas watch, checking the time again for no good reason. Zach was gone. He'd never get to see his nieces' gift for him or the Stetson she bought. Why hadn't she stopped him?

"Did you ever wonder why Steve's will had that silly RangePro clause?"

"Huh? What?" Stunned, Emma turned to stare at her sister.

"Why did Steve—"

"I heard you. Yes. I think about it often. Usually at 2:00 a.m. Long ago, I came to the conclusion that deep down inside he didn't trust me to run his company, otherwise why didn't he tell me about this addendum to his will?"

"I'm sure that wasn't it at all. And if it was,

well, you proved him wrong the last three years, haven't you?"

"Why do *you* think he did it?" Emma asked. The teakettle began to whistle, and she jumped up. "I've got this."

"I think Steve wanted to create a valid and compelling reason why Zach eventually had to come back. He wanted Zach to look out for you in case anything happened to him. I really believe Steve wanted to unite the people he cared for in the event of his death."

"I don't know, Luce. That seems a stretch," Emma said as she carefully filled the mugs with hot water. She returned the kettle to the stove and faced Lucy.

"Emma, do you think that Steve was aware that Zach cared for you?"

"I hope and pray that my husband didn't think I cared for anyone but him."

"That's not what I asked." Lucy placed a comforting hand on Emma's arm. "Your heart is pure and so is Zach's. That's why Zach stayed away. He would never do anything dishonorable. Ever. That's not the kind of man he is. At the same time, it doesn't prevent him from having feelings for you."

Emma sank into the chair and wrapped her hand around the hot mug. "Oh, Lucy. If you're right..." Emma released a breath. And she suspected her sister was. "Then what kind of person am I if I didn't even realize Zach harbored feelings for me?"

"This is Zach, Em. They coined the term 'strong and silent type' when he was born. The man holds his cards so close to his chest even he can't read them."

"I'm so confused. What if I had known back then? Would I have chosen Zach over Steve?"

Lucy gave an adamant shake of her head. "You can't go there. We both know too well that trying to rewrite the past is a dangerous game. Every single day we have an obligation to live a life that asks, 'What's on the agenda today, Lord?' You, Travis and I have done that to the best of our ability with our lives and with Big Heart Ranch."

She pulled her tea bag from the mug and looked at Emma. "Sure, we have a ton of unanswered questions. The journey has definitely not been easy, or without obstacles. That's why it's called faith."

"I know you're right, but I'm so overwhelmed with everything… I didn't sleep a bit last night." Emma raised a hand in gesture. "I don't know what to say, Lucy."

"You don't have to say anything. I just want you to see this situation another way and maybe consider the possibility that RangePro is standing between you and Zach."

"Consider? I admit it! That's the reason Zach left."

"Isn't there another way you can honor Steve?"

Emma blinked. "Another way?"

Lucy scooted her chair closer and took Emma's hand. "Do you think Rachel and Elizabeth will care about a software company called RangePro when they grow up?"

"I thought they might. I mean, I keep remembering the way everything was taken away from us when we went into foster care."

"That was wrong. I'm so sorry that was part of your childhood." Lucy wiped at a trail of moisture sliding down her face. "I wish I could have done something."

"Lucy, you were twelve years old."

"That's the only thing that keeps me sane when I remember that dark time."

They sat in silence for a moment holding each other's hands tightly.

"Em, surely you realize that what we went through isn't the same as selling RangePro."

"Do I? I don't think I'm there yet."

"Okay, let's take it a step further. Why not take the money and run? You've put enough sweat equity into the company since Steve died. It's worth whatever Randall is willing to pay and it sounds like he's willing to pay handsomely."

"That's a lot of money. What would I do with all that money?"

"Give Zach his half and find something that will remind the girls that their daddy was an amazing man."

Emma's eyes widened as she considered the idea. "Oh, Lucy, you're brilliant."

Lucy grinned and patted herself on the back. "You know, I keep telling Jack that, but he's not been as receptive to the concept as you are."

"I'll call Beau Randall on Monday." Once again, she glanced at her watch. "Zach is probably halfway to California by now."

"He hasn't left."

"What? How do you know that?"

"I sent Dutch out in the snow to find out. Oh, and I sent him with your Christmas presents for Zach. I thought that might tug a few heartstrings in your favor."

Emma went to the doorway and peeked into Lucy's living room. Her gaze scanned the family's decorated Virginia pine. The gifts Emma had brought for Zach were missing from beneath the graceful branches. "I can't believe you did that without asking me."

"No thanks are necessary. I'm sure you'd do the same for me if the situation was reversed."

Lucy stood behind Emma. "What do you think of my tree?"

"It's very nice, but I won. Zach went with me and we cut ours a week ago." Zach had decorated her tree, too. More memories to haunt her daydreams.

"That's only because I'm a little slow with the kiddo on board. I'll win next year." Suddenly, Lucy grimaced, and her hand shot to her lower back and then to her abdomen. "Ouch. That one hurt."

"You're having contractions?" Emma squeaked.

"Yes. They started a bit ago."

"Why didn't you say something? Grab your bag. Let's get going."

"Oh, I'm not going anywhere until absolutely necessary. The last time we went to the hospital they made me hang around for hours while they timed my contractions and poked at me and then they sent me home."

"Jack!"

"No! Emma, do not call him. If I say the word *contraction*, he gets short of breath and needs a brown paper bag. He'll try to find an Uber again."

"An Uber in Timber, Oklahoma?"

"I know." She shook her head.

Emma reached for her purse. "I'm calling AJ and Travis. They're probably on the way anyhow. They can stay with the kids. I'll be the designated driver."

"Oh, Emma. Is this really necessary?"

"Unless you're planning to give birth on the dining room table, yes, it is. *Am I the only rational adult in this house?*" She pulled back the blinds, tangling the cord as she did. "And the snow continues. Maybe we should call an ambulance." Emma turned and walked straight into a wall.

"Now who's rational?" Lucy sipped her tea.

"Jack!" Emma yelled as she rubbed her head. "I wish Zach was here. He's good in emergencies. He'd know exactly what to do."

"Oh, I'm sure our humble hero will be along soon enough."

"I wish I had as much faith in Dutch as you do." Emma scooped up her coat and grabbed her boots.

"Dutch is not my rock. The good Lord has had His hand on the Maxwell children for a long time. He won't let us down. Your navy SEAL will be back where he belongs before you know it."

"In the meantime, Lucy, would you please get your coat and overnight bag? I'll grab Christmas cookies for the nursing staff." Emma stopped and stared at her sister. "You're really going to have a Christmas baby!"

Zach sat in a corner booth of the Timber diner that overlooked Main Street, nursing his fourth cup of coffee. Outside, fat flakes of snow rode through the air on the back of a strong northerly gust. The holiday flags on the streetlamps flapped back and forth, waving a greeting.

Emma's flags.

Everything reminded him of Emma.

"We're going to close soon, son." A smiling gray-haired waitress stopped by his table. "I can give you a to-go cup if you like."

"I'm good. Thanks very much." He pulled out his wallet and slipped a ten under the white mug.

"The coffee was only two bucks."

"It's almost Christmas," he said.

She smiled. "So it is. You have a wonderful holiday."

"Yeah," he murmured. A wonderful holiday. Christmas Eve and he was like Ebenezer Scrooge, taking a glimpse into his own future. All he saw was a string of lonely all-night diners and a vision of himself running from what he should have had instead of grabbing what he could have.

He had been sitting in the Timber Diner for hours because he lacked the courage to move on, or the guts to go tell Emma he loved her.

Zach stood and reached for his coat. Shrugging his arms into the sleeves, he headed for the door.

"Don't forget your hat."

He examined the pristine black Stetson hanging on the hook outside the booth. Where had it come from? He'd been the only patron in the diner for the last few hours. "That's not my hat."

"Sure it is. Dutch Stevens came in and said you left it behind. He put it there when you were in the restroom. I got so busy cleaning the grill that I forgot to tell you." She pointed outside. "Dutch's truck's still out there."

Dutch came out in this weather to bring him a hat? Zach pulled the Stetson from the peg. Tucked inside was a wrapped Christmas package with his name on it. This was beyond strange. Even for Dutch.

Zach carefully slipped the package into his pocket. Hand on the Stetson's crown, he ran his fingers over the brim before he placed the hat on his head. The Stetson fit like it was made for him.

"Thank you, ma'am." He walked past the cash register, his knee aching from the dip in barometric pressure. At the counter, he noticed a display of what Dutch would call geegaws. Dangly Christmas earrings, little red and green beaded bracelets and ridiculous necklaces. Zach couldn't help but smile as he fingered a sparkly necklace of tiny holiday lights.

"I'd like to buy this."

"Cute, isn't it?" She held it up and smiled. "Gift?"

"Yeah."

"I'll take off the price tag for you." She slipped the necklace into the bag and then reached to the display and picked up a silver candy cane ring as well. "The ring is on the house."

Zach smiled as he slid the money across the counter and took the white bag. "Thanks again."

"You're welcome. Be careful out there. Lots of accidents tonight."

"Yes, ma'am." Pulling out his keys, Zach pushed open the glass door and stood on the sidewalk looking up and down the street as snow continued to fall, covering the town in a comforter of white. Sure enough, Dutch's beat-up pickup was parked along the street. Except, the old wrangler wasn't in it.

The streets of Timber were all but empty on Christmas Eve. His footsteps on the snowy ground echoed with each step into the night.

When the wind sliced through him, Zach zipped the barn coat and dug in his pockets for gloves.

He stared at his truck. A thick coating of ice covered most of the windows, and he didn't even have a scraper. There wasn't a need for one in San Diego.

The driver's-side door was nearly glued shut with ice, and it took a few minutes for him to pick away at the frozen moisture so he could climb into the cab. Inside wasn't much better. Frigid air blasted him from the vents. While the truck worked on the seemingly impossible mission of warming things up, he pulled the Christmas package from his pocket. Emma had printed in her neat writing on the colorful tag. "To Unca Zach, love Rachel and Bit."

He carefully peeled back the paper. A homemade Popsicle stick frame colored by the girls and decorated with stars and glitter held a picture of himself with Rachel and Elizabeth decorating Emma's Christmas tree. His fingers touched the photo as though he could bring back that particular moment in time.

But he couldn't. It was gone.

Zach closed his eyes tight against the pain that kicked him straight in the gut. He sat in the dark truck, beneath the light of a streetlamp, shivering as the heaters cranked out less than warm air.

Forgiveness and trust. The words drifted through his mind. He'd expected it and hadn't been willing to offer the same in return. Zach pulled out his cell phone and scrolled through the contacts, knowing what he needed to do.

Despite his claims to the contrary, he'd kept up with his mother, though he rarely contacted her. He swallowed and depressed the call button, steeling himself against more rejection.

Voice mail.

"Um, Mom, this is Zach. Merry Christmas."

He pushed End and relaxed against the seat. It was a start.

A knock on his window a moment later had Zach jumping. All he could see was a dark shadow through the ice-coated window.

"Open the door."

Dutch.

Zach stepped outside and shivered some more.

"It's minus six degrees out here. You sitting here for fun?" Dutch asked. Snowflakes clung to the old cowboy's handlebar mustache and his nose was bright red.

"Where did you come from, Rudolph?"

"Down the street, yonder. Had to make a few stops before I head out to the airport." He grinned. "My sweetheart's back in town. Next stop is the Tulsa airport to pick her up. What's your excuse?"

"I'm pretty much out of excuses," Zach admitted. "Got any words of wisdom?"

"Seems pretty clear to me." Dutch blew a long breath of air into his cupped hands and rubbed them together.

"Does it?"

"Yessiree. I can explain it to you, Zach, but I can't understand it for you." Dutch stared at the Stetson and gave a slow nod. "Nice hat."

"You got me a hat."

"In your dreams. The hat's courtesy of Miss Emma."

"Emma?"

"Sure enough. Miss Lucy gave it to me to pass along to you. Told me it's a Christmas present from her sister. And that's all I know."

"Apparently not. You knew I was here. How'd you figure that out?"

Dutch snorted. "You brokenhearted cowboys are all the same. You run, but you don't ride away."

"Is that right?"

"Yep. I knew you weren't leaving town until the end of the month. You promised Travis and you're a man of your word. Figured you'd be wallowing in your coffee somewhere." A dry chuckle slipped from his lips. "Called that one, didn't I?"

Zach pulled his collar up against the blowing snow and shoved his hands deep into his pockets. "Is…" He paused.

"Spit it out, I ain't got all night."

"Is Emma at the Harris's tonight?"

"Naw, she's on the way to the hospital with Lucy."

"The hospital?" Adrenaline zipped through him like a Taser.

Dutch's phone beeped and the cowboy juggled the device, nearly dropping the cell before he read the text. "I gotta go. Plane landed. I'm forty-five minutes from the airport." The old cowboy gave a giddy chuckle and turned toward his pickup. "Who'da thunk?" he mumbled. "Planes never arrive early on Christmas Eve."

"Wait, Dutch. Which hospital?"

"Pawhuska's the closest one."

"Pawhuska?"

"You got a hearing problem? You keep repeating everything I say." Dutch opened his truck door and reached into the glove box. "Might need a scraper."

He tossed it through the air and Zach caught the plastic tool.

"Thanks."

"Sure thing."

"Dutch, why is Emma going to the hospital?"

"Do I look like a doctor to you?" he called through the open window of his truck. The old pickup backfired a few times before the engine purred. "You'll have to ask her."

"Are the twins okay?"

"Far as I know."

"And Lucy?"

"Lucy looked fine the last time I saw her, but I can't be expected to keep up with everyone, and I sure can't jaw with you any longer. Rue is coming in and my nose is about frozen."

Zach nodded. "Merry Christmas, Dutch."

"Back at you, cowboy." He pointed a finger at Zach. "You know what you gotta do. You're a smart fella. Navy SEAL and all. You'll figure it out."

"Navy SEAL and all," Zach muttered as Dutch's truck pulled away.

Zach began to scrape ice from the windows, leaning into the job, as he thought about Dutch's words. Travis would tell him what was going on.

Zach pulled out his cell and punched in Travis's number. The call went straight to voice mail.

"The Pawhuska hospital it is."

The wipers beat a steady nonstop rhythm as they pushed the wet snow from his windshield. Poor visibility had him crawling down State Highway 99 to Pawhuska, relying on his headlights to find the road buried in white.

"You got your white Christmas, Emma," he murmured.

Traffic was scarce, not even trucks on a holiday evening. Twenty minutes down the road and he spotted a minivan pulled to the side with its flashers on. A distress flare flickered at a distance from the vehicle.

Minivan. That meant a family. He had to stop.

Zach got out of the truck and frowned. The snow had stopped. Overhead, the sky was clear with a blanket of stars tossed across the darkness. The air wore the perfume of pine mixed with a trace of diesel and asphalt.

Zach approached the vehicle from the rear with cautious steps, due to the ice, while assessing the ground. One set of footsteps was still visible from the vehicle to the flare, telling him the minivan had pulled over recently. Zach knocked snow from the license plate, snapped a picture and slipped his phone back into his pocket. His thumb hovered over the emergency icon as he continued to the driver's-side window.

He offered a soft knuckle tap and stood back, ready to move if necessary. The driver's-side window descended a few inches.

"You folks need some help?"

"*Zach?* Is that you?"

"Emma?" he said her name, swallowing unspoken relief at seeing her in the driver's seat.

"Zach, what are you doing here?" The window quickly opened and her breath turned into small clouds of cold air.

"Dutch said you were at the hospital. I was headed that way."

"Lucy. The baby."

"I thought it was you."

"I'm not having a baby." She chuckled.

"I thought you were sick or something."

"I'm fine."

Emma was fine. His gaze held hers for a long moment.

The nearest rear passenger window descended and Jack Harris stuck his head out. "Zach. You're an answer to prayer. Thanks for stopping."

"Sure thing, Jack. How's Lucy?"

"Another contraction," Lucy called out from the back seat. Her voice was tight with discomfort.

Zach grimaced. "What's wrong with the vehicle?"

"I'm not sure," Jack returned. "I called 9-1-1 but there are crashes all over due to the road conditions. Response time is abysmal. We're on a wait list for a tow from the only garage still open. Christmas Eve and nobody is working."

"We can do better than that. Let's get Lucy into the truck before I have to deliver the baby."

Jack paled at the words. "Good idea."

Emma opened the driver's-side door and stepped out. "Oops." Her feet scissored, sliding back and forth on the snow that had turned to ice. When she pitched forward, Zach wrapped his arms around her.

"I've got you."

"Your leg."

"Is fine. I've got you, Emma."

She leaned against him. "Oh, Zach. I'm so glad you didn't leave."

"Me, too," he whispered against her hair.

His gaze went to the starry sky and he remembered her words from yesterday. *A time of new beginnings. Like the birth of our Lord at Christmas.*

It was a second chance to make things right. Armed with all the reasons that he had fallen in love with Emma, Zach promised himself that this time he would fight for the future he wanted.

Chapter Thirteen

"Mr. Norman, you and your wife can go in and visit now. Congratulations. The little fellow is our first Christmas baby of the year."

"Thank you."

He downed the rest of his coffee and tossed the cup into a trash can. "My wife," he mused. Zach repeated the words yet again, allowing himself to wrap his wildest dreams around them. But then, he'd always dreamed big.

A glance out the window of the waiting room had him pausing to admire the midnight sky. The Shepard's Star shined with a steady glow surrounded by millions of twinkling lights. This was quite the ending to his eight weeks' of holiday indoctrination at Big Heart Ranch.

Across the room, a dozing Emma changed position in the hard plastic waiting room chair. She had been sleeping on and off the last few hours while they waited for the okay to visit Lucy and Jack and their newborn baby boy.

The waiting room was otherwise empty, allowing him to do nothing but think while she slept. He drank endless cups of coffee from the vending machine while reviewing the path that brought him to now.

The few instances his gaze had connected with Emma's since they arrived had been awkward. Several times he thought she was about to say something, then she drew back and turned away.

That moment in the snow out on Highway 99, she'd said that she was glad he hadn't left, but was that only because of Lucy?

Zach couldn't blame her. He'd let Emma down from day one, three years ago when Steve died. Though he tried making it up to her these last weeks, the RangePro situation left him eating dust, and he didn't know how to make things right.

"Emma," he called.

"Hmm?" Her head bobbed, as she fought sleep like Rachel and Elizabeth at the dinner table.

"The nurse said you can go in now."

"What?" Suddenly Emma was wide-awake. She met his gaze from across the room.

"You can go in and see the baby. The nurse said they're ready."

"Thank you." She stood and stretched her

shoulders and then turned to him and frowned. "Aren't you going in?"

"This is family visiting."

"Zach, you're family. You've always been family and you will never stop being family." She put her hands on her hips. "Why is it you don't get that?"

"I get it now." He stared at her for a moment before following her to the birthing suite.

They washed their hands and Emma turned to him. "Do I look like I've been sleeping in a chair?"

"No, but why is there a bruise on your forehead?"

"I ran into a wall." She raised a hand. "Don't ask."

"I'm afraid to." Zach knocked on the door.

"Come on in," Jack said.

The room was huge, with not only a bed, but also a couch and a rocking chair. There was even a Roman tub with a Jacuzzi. It was like nothing Zach had ever seen before.

Lucy sat propped against pillows holding a swaddled infant, who wore a tiny red-and-white knitted Santa cap.

"Congratulations," Emma cried. She hugged Jack, kissed her sister and fussed over the baby.

"Did you hear?" Lucy asked. "The first Christmas baby for the hospital. They took a picture for the newspaper and I asked them to fax the article to the *Timber Independence.* We're going to milk our five minutes of fame."

"As you should," Emma said. "You did nine months of hard labor."

"I did, didn't I?"

"Yes," Emma said with a nod. "Where did that darling hat come from?"

"The nurse brought it in. I suspect I'm their favorite patient because you put cookies and candy canes in the staff lounge."

"Lucy, you're their only patient, but a little Christmas cheer can't hurt, especially since they're working on a holiday."

Jack met Zach at the door. "I know I've said it half a dozen times already, Zach, but thanks for being a Good Samaritan tonight. I knew the Lord was watching over us, but I had no idea He'd send a navy SEAL."

"Congratulations," Zach said, shaking the new father's hand.

"Have you called Travis and AJ?" Emma asked.

Jack held up a computer notebook. "We've FaceTimed with them and the kids. For once, Lucy is impressed with all my techno gadgets."

"Dub and the girls got to see the baby already thanks to Jack's toys," Lucy said.

"What did Dub say?" Emma asked.

"That little guy is so excited. He can't wait for his brother to come home," Jack said.

"Come closer, you two," Lucy said. "I want you to officially meet Daniel Zachary Harris."

Zach's head jerked up. "Who?"

"Daniel Zachary Harris. Daniel for Jack's brother and Zachary after you," Lucy explained. "Thanks to you, he wasn't born on the road to Pawhuska."

"All I did was drive my pickup."

"Emma, can you please explain to the navy SEAL that he's a hero?"

"I'll try, Lucy, but this is just another day for Zach."

"Not to us," Jack said. "You and Zach helped bring little Daniel Zachary safely into the world on Christmas Day, and we'd like you both to be the baby's godparents."

Zach opened his mouth and closed it again. Jack's and Lucy's words touched him deeply. His heart ached with a joy he didn't even understand. Speechless, he shoved his hands in his pockets.

"We'd be honored. Right, Zach?" Emma prompted.

"Yeah." The word was husky with emotion.

"Come here, Zach," Lucy said. "Time to take a good look at your godchild."

Zach moved closer to the bed, more nervous now than when he was shipping out on a new mission.

Standing next to Emma, he prayed no one

would notice his trembling hands as he stared with wonder at the infant nestled in the blanket.

"Tiny little thing," Zach murmured.

"Tiny and wondrous," Emma said softly.

The miniature hand broke free of the swaddling and reached out to him. When Zach touched the delicate fist with his index finger, the infant wrapped his fingers around Zach's big one.

For minutes, the room was silent as hearts overflowed for a baby who was only hours old. Zach lifted his head and Emma was smiling at him, her eyes moist. Her expression said that she, too, would be tucking this amazing memory away.

"Hello?" A smiling middle-aged woman peeked her head in the room.

"Rue? Is that you?" Lucy cried as the door opened further.

"It's me. I can't believe you had the baby without me. What were you thinking?" Dutch's sweetheart pushed gray curls away from her face and her eyes fanned the room as she entered.

"Looks like we've got our own live nativity here," Dutch said from the doorway.

"Have you just promoted yourself to a wise man, Dutch?" Rue asked. The sturdy retired general and physician stepped up to Zach and held out her hand. "You must be Zach Norman. Dutch has been telling me all about you."

"Pleased to meet you, ma'am." He took the

woman's offered hand and nodded. "Heard a lot about you, too."

She rolled her eyes. "Don't believe anything he tells you. Our Dutch is quite loquacious."

"Yes, ma'am. He is."

"Hey there," Dutch protested. "Speak English if you're gonna insult me."

Rue laughed and moved to hug Emma. "Oh, my dear, you and I have some catching up to do."

"You've been missed, Rue," Emma said. "Dutch has been out of control since you've been gone."

"Hey, I resemble that remark," Dutch said as he sidled up to Zach.

Zach narrowed his eyes at the old cowboy.

"I see you found your way back home."

"Navy SEALS don't get lost," Zach returned.

"Aw, sure they do. They just don't tell anyone."

Zach turned and pinned him with his gaze. "Did you know that Lucy was having the baby?"

"Might have heard something about it." Dutch shrugged. "Things turned out fine, didn't they?"

Zach shot Dutch a menacing look, and the cowboy inched away and turned to Emma.

"Everything's fine here, right, Miss Emma?"

"Right, Dutch. Absolutely, right. Whatever you said."

"See, there," Dutch said to Zach.

When Dutch and Rue moved closer to see the

baby, Zach took the opportunity to grab his Stetson from a chair and slip out the door. He pulled his keys from his pocket. Time to get going. Emma could easily get a ride home.

Halfway down the hall, he stopped. What was he doing?

"Can I help you, sir?" a nurse asked.

"No, I'm good, thanks."

"You looked lost for a moment there."

"Yeah. I guess I was."

Zach shook his head. He'd promised himself he was going to fight for his future and here he was running away again. No more.

He turned around and sidestepped when he realized Emma was right behind him.

"We need to talk," she said.

"Yeah, we do."

Surprise flickered in her eyes. "Where were you going?"

"Nowhere. Absolutely nowhere. And I was taking a shortcut to get there."

"You weren't leaving?"

"Not me."

"Come on." She grabbed his hand and headed down the hospital corridor.

He almost asked where she was going. Then he realized that it didn't matter. He'd follow Emma anywhere. Yeah, from here on in, she was going to have a hard time getting rid of him.

* * *

Emma pushed open the door to the hospital's chapel and paused for a moment inside the room. Stained-glass windows lined the wall behind a small altar that held fat golden pillars. Recessed lighting gave the room a golden warm glow.

"It's beautiful in here," Emma murmured.

"'For those who seek solace and peace,'" Zach said, reading the inscription on the wall behind the altar. "I'm ready for that."

"Are you?" Emma asked quietly.

"Yes."

Emma slid into a pew and Zach followed. She bowed her head for a moment, allowing the stress of the last few days to ease from her shoulders. It wasn't her burden. No, it was the Lord's. Silently offering a prayer for the outcome of the next minutes, she reached for Zach's hand.

"I'm sorry, Zach," she said.

"For what?"

"For not trusting you to honor my opinion about RangePro when you went into that meeting. I hounded you into your involvement with RangePro and then challenged your handling of Beau Randall." She cringed. "I even accused you of being part of his schemes. I blamed you for everything when all you were trying to do was protect me."

"It's okay, Emma."

"Stop being so nice. It's not okay. It's never okay to treat the people you love like that. I'm a therapist. I should know better."

Zach's eyes widened. "Say that again?"

"I'm a therapist?"

"No. Not that part."

Emma smiled. "Oh, that part. Zach, you know I care for you."

"Do you? Am I Zach your friend and neighbor? Did we become good buddies again, or what exactly?"

"Would it be okay if I run the meeting agenda?"

He laughed. "I expect nothing less from you. Go for it."

"About RangePro."

"That's what you want to lead with?"

"Yes, because this is what has stood between us. RangePro is the last material reminder of Steve. It has been difficult for me to let go, and I've clung to the company for all the wrong reasons because of my own baggage. I've come to realize that memories are important but living for today is even more important." She swallowed. "Steve will always hold a place in my heart. Always. But it's time for me to move forward."

"Emma, whatever you want to do is fine by me."

"Perfect, because I'm selling."

His eyes rounded. "Selling?"

"To Beau Randall, and I'm going to get a better price and a charitable donation to the Steve Norman Big Heart Ranch Scholarship Fund from that rhinestone cowboy while I'm at it."

"A scholarship fund?"

"A scholarship for children of Big Heart Ranch who are pursuing mathematics and science degrees based on need and academics."

"Emma." Zach breathed her name like a prayer. "Steve would be proud of you. This truly honors my brother. I want my half of the funds to go one hundred percent to the scholarship."

"You do?"

"Yeah. It's a great idea, and don't forget to tap my father for a hefty contribution." He grinned. "The clients of RangePro will no doubt be happy to donate, as well."

"Jack handles contract law and is in-house counsel for the Brisbane Foundation. I'm sure he'll take care of everything. Pro bono even, since we are the Christmas baby's godparents."

"I'll even let him call me a hero if it will benefit the scholarship fund."

"Zach, you are a hero. Accept it gracefully. You were sent to Big Heart Ranch to be our hero."

"I'm not so sure about that, but I am willing to find out what's next, now that the Holiday Roundup is completed."

"What's next is renting a cherry picker again to take down all those decorations."

"And then?"

"There's always something going on at Big Heart Ranch, Zach. I'm sure you've figured that out by now. Are you thinking about staying on?"

"Oh, I'm not leaving, Emma. I want to make that clear. No matter what the future holds, I'm sticking around."

"I've wanted to hear those words for eight weeks."

"If we both weren't so stubborn we might have held this meeting last week."

"Today is Christmas. I believe our timing is perfect."

"Do you think Travis will want another wrangler?"

"We vet all candidates. You probably have an unfair advantage with the staff, since Lucy, Travis, Tripp and I all have plans for your future on Big Heart Ranch."

"I'll take that advantage, and I've got a few plans of my own."

"You do?" Emma smiled at the excitement in Zach's gray eyes.

"I want to involve Joe and Mary Clark. They have years of knowledge and so much love to share."

"Big Heart Ranch always needs more grandparents. They're retired farmers, too. Maybe they could help us launch our community garden."

"Another great Emma plan." He took a deep

breath and met her gaze. "Speaking of grandparents, I called my mother."

Emma released a small gasp. "Zach."

"She didn't pick up, but I left a message."

"It's a start."

He nodded. "Is there anything else on the agenda?"

"Yes. One more thing." She turned to him. "Do you have any questions before we proceed?"

"Only one. Would it be okay to kiss the beautiful woman running this meeting?"

"Yes. Kisses are expected and appreciated."

Emma slid closer to Zach, her heart skipping as his lips touched hers. He delivered a sweet kiss full of promises and then leaned in for another.

"Wait," Emma said with a hand to his chest. "I think I might be doing this all wrong."

"I thought you were doing fine," Zach said with a wink.

"You haven't told me how you feel."

"Isn't that obvious?"

"I need to hear the words."

"Emma, I've loved you all my life. When Steve was with us, it seemed a betrayal. When we lost him, things became even more complicated. I stayed away because I didn't know what to do…"

"And now?"

"Is there room in your heart for me?"

"So much room. My heart is growing larger each day with the thought of all the memories we're going to make. I know that Steve would want me to be happy. You make me happy."

"How can I possibly make you happy? You are like this radiant light. A star shooting across the sky. What do I have to offer you?"

"You could start with your love, Zach."

"You have that. You've always had that."

Emma took his hands. "That's all I need. Your unconditional love."

"You really want to hitch yourself to a broken-down former navy SEAL?"

"I want you by my side for the rest of our lives. If that's one day, or two, or a thousand."

Zach grinned. "This meeting is going much better than I'd anticipated. The only downside is you didn't bring chocolate muffins."

"I'll remember for the next meeting."

"Will there be more meetings?" he asked.

"Oh, yes, Zach. Many, many more."

His cell phone buzzed and he pulled it out of his pocket. When he did, the white bag fell out and he grabbed it and placed it on the pew next to his Stetson. Zach held up the phone. "It's Lucy. Should I answer?"

"The mother of the Christmas baby. I suppose we should." Emma smiled. "Give me your phone." He handed it to her, and she fiddled with it before holding it out at arm's length. "Now kiss me."

"Yes, ma'am."

The camera flashed.

"I'll send that to her and she'll leave us alone for a while longer."

Zach laughed.

"What's in the bag?" Emma asked.

"Christmas present." He pulled the necklace out of the bag and flicked the tiny switch that started the lights blinking. "For you."

Emma slipped it over her head and arranged the gaudy necklace on her red sweater. "It's beautiful, and it matches my watch."

"Not nearly as good as the Stetson and the picture of the girls you gave me. Thank you, Emma."

"You're welcome." She looked up into his eyes and smiled. "You gave me Christmas cheer. That would have never happened eight weeks ago."

He raised a brow. "True. I've changed."

Zach put a hand to the back of the pew in front of him and carefully eased to a kneeling position, thankful for thick carpeting.

"What are you doing?" Emma sputtered.

"One more present." Zach reached in the bag for the candy cane ring. "Emma Maxwell Norman, I love you. Will you marry me?"

"Oh, Zach. I love the ring."

"Yeah, but do you love it enough to marry me?"

"Oh, yes. Yes. I will marry you."

He slipped the ring on her finger and kissed her palm.

"It's Christmas. Let's go home to our little family and celebrate."

Zach carefully got to his feet and pressed his lips to hers. "Merry Christmas, Emma."

"Merry Christmas, Zach."

Epilogue

"Emma, let's get married," Zach Norman said. He pulled his Stetson from his head and wiped his face with a bandanna. Arms folded over the horse stall, he watched her tack Rodeo.

Emma tugged the glove on her left hand off with her teeth and wiggled her fingers at him. "That's a wonderful idea, but I'm already married." The modest diamond solitaire sparkled on her finger.

Zach leaned over the gate and met his wife's lips for a sweet kiss.

"Aw, are you two smooching again?" Dutch strode past, his boots clomping and his expression agitated. "I'd have never meddled if I knew I was gonna have to put up with this romantic stuff."

"We like smooching," Zach returned.

The cowboy snorted loudly. "You seen Travis?"

"Travis went to town with AJ for a checkup. You know their baby is due this summer."

Dutch raised his hands into the air. "Babies everywhere I look. We've got cattle ready to drop in the paddock. Those are the only babies I'm interested in at the moment."

"Do you need help?" Emma asked.

"Why, yes. Matter of fact, I could use a hand or two. We've only got a hundred head or so out there." He shook his head. "Nice of you to ask."

"We'll be there shortly," Zach called as the grumpy wrangler stomped out.

Zach turned back to Emma. "So what do you think about renewing our vows at Christmas? Right before the next Holiday Roundup. It'll be nearly our one-year anniversary."

"That's a very romantic thought, Zach."

"Yeah. It was your sister's idea. She also said to thank you for the chocolate muffins." He frowned. "You made chocolate muffins?"

"They're on the counter. You had already left to take the girls to preschool. I pulled them out of the oven before I headed to town this morning and dropped off some at the admin building."

"There are dozens of reasons why I love you, Emma, but your chocolate muffins are in the top ten."

Emma chuckled. "Thank you."

His phone beeped, and he pulled the cell from the pocket of his Wranglers. "Text from Jack. The official documentation has been filed and approved for the Steve Norman Scholarship Fund

Foundation. We'll have the first award announcement at the Timber High School commencement in May."

"Oh, Zach. That's wonderful. Wow, May. That's only two and a half months away."

"You'll be presenting the scholarship, Emma. We'll bring the girls to watch."

"Steve would have been proud and someday Rachel and Elizabeth will understand this legacy of their father that we've created."

Zach nodded in agreement.

"We did a good thing, didn't we?" Emma asked with a slight hesitation in her voice.

"Yes, sweetheart, we did."

Emma blinked and a shimmery drop of moisture slipped from her dark lashes.

Zach unlocked the stall and pulled her into his arms. "You okay?"

"Yes," she said, resting her head against his chest. "I'm just getting emotional again. Seems to happen a lot lately."

"As long as you're happy, you can get as emotional as you want."

She sniffed. "Oh, Zach. I'm very happy."

"Me, too. And the wedding in December idea? Renewing our vows in the gazebo beneath those LED lights Mick and Benjie and I will have strung by then. What do you think? I've always thought we should have gotten married during your favorite season."

"Normally, I'd be all over that, but we have a prior commitment for December." She stepped back and met his gaze. A soft and tender smile touched her mouth.

"We do? I don't remember that." He frowned, trying to recall. "Did Lucy or Travis schedule something?"

"No, you and I have inadvertently made plans."

"We have?" He shook his head. "What sort of plans?"

"I saw that new doctor in Timber today."

"Yeah. How'd that go? I ran into her at the Timber General Store. Told me she has a colleague who's doing some innovative work in orthopedics. Gave me his card."

"Really? Your knee?"

"Worth checking out, right?"

"Absolutely." Emma reached for the oats.

"Your exam went okay?" Zach asked. He took the sack of oats from her arms. "Let me get that."

"I did have some unexpected news," she murmured.

His hand slipped as he filled the trough and he dropped the sack. Rodeo gave a little blow of air and a snort of disapproval.

"Sorry, pal." Zach turned to his wife and took her hands in his. "Whatever it is, I'm here for you."

"Zach, I don't know how else to tell you this."

"Tell me what?" A tiny shiver danced down his

arms and he blinked with the sudden realization that he knew exactly what she was going to say.

"We're going to have a baby."

He grabbed the stall gate for support.

"Sit down, Zach, before you fall down."

"No. I'm fine." He leaned against the metal gate and worked to gather his thoughts.

"You're awfully pale. Are you okay?"

"The truth is, I'm not okay. I'm over the moon." He pulled off the Stetson and ran a hand through his hair before perching it on the back of his head. "I'm also hyperventilating, but I'm definitely happy."

Emma put her small hand on the side of his face and reached up to touch her lips to his.

"A baby?" He repeated the words against her mouth.

"Yes. In nine months. That's how it works."

Zach tugged her close. Close enough to wrap his arms around his cowgirl.

"You smell like chocolate muffins," he whispered against her hair.

"Do I?" She offered a soft laugh and then sighed.

"Thank you, Emma."

"For what?"

"For loving me back. For reminding me how much I have to be thankful for."

"He's healed our hearts and expanded our territories," she said. "We have our own family now and our extended family on Big Heart Ranch."

Zach nodded in complete agreement.

Was it possible that he loved Emma even more today than last December in that little hospital chapel on Christmas morning when the Lord had given him a new beginning? He closed his eyes and inhaled the sweet scent of home. Hay, horses and his wife.

The year ahead held only more opportunities for a future filled with joy, and another holiday baby at Big Heart Ranch.

* * * * *

If you loved this story, pick up the other books in the Big Heart Ranch series from beloved author Tina Radcliffe:

Claiming Her Cowboy
Falling for the Cowgirl

Available now from Love Inspired!

Dear Reader,

I'm so delighted to return to Big Heart Ranch in Timber, Oklahoma. What a treat it was to weave a story of faith and love at the most wondrous time of the year, Christmas. A time when we celebrate the birth of our Lord.

This third installment introduces you to the third and youngest Maxwell, Emma Maxwell Norman. Along with her siblings, Lucy and Travis, Emma manages Big Heart Ranch for orphaned, abused and neglected children, where unconditional love and the good Lord reign. Widowed Emma carries the additional challenge of being a single mother to twin daughters.

A former navy SEAL with a troubled past, Zach Norman returns to Timber and lands right in Emma's path. He's the only man who can possibly win the heart of the fiercely independent whirlwind of a cowgirl. Zach and Emma must learn to trust and set aside their fears in order to find their happy ending. And isn't that the way it always works? We must let go of the past to grab the future the Lord has for us.

I hope you enjoy this romantic and inspirational holiday tale. Do drop me a note and let me know your thoughts. I can be reached through my website, www.tinaradcliffe.com, where you can also find Emma's chocolate muffin recipe.

Sincerely,
Tina Radcliffe